This Country of Mine

This Country of Mine

by Didier Leclair

Translated by
Elaine Kennedy

Deux Voiliers Publishing
Aylmer, Quebec

First Edition 2018

English translation copyright © Elaine Kennedy

ISBN 978-1-928049-52-4 (Ingram edition)

Original French © Didier Leclair

Translation of original work by Didier Leclair published in French as *Ce pays qui est le mien* by Les Éditions du Vermillon, 2003.

First English edition of chapter one, "It's Late, Doctor Schweitzer," published by *carte blanche* in winter 2014.

English-translation revisor: Lee Heppner

French-language consultant: Pénélope Mallard

Published in Canada by

Deux Voiliers Publishing, Aylmer, Quebec.

www.deuxvoilierspublishing.com

Cover Design – Ian Thomas Shaw

For Perpétue Mukantabana or Peggy — DL

❧❧❧❧

For Andrew — EK

I

It's Late, Doctor Schweitzer

THE NIGHT WAS a coal-black mass covered with a thick white blanket. The snow falling gently over Toronto was forcing motorists to slow down. Most were unable to prevent their vehicles from sliding, as they weren't accustomed to the slippery buildup. Usually the snow eased off and melted quickly enough from the pavement. On the east side of the city, in an apartment on Sutton Street, an exhausted couple lay sleeping. Apollinaire Mavoungou and his wife Adèle lived in a tiny furnished basement with their baby. Their slumberous faces were those of depleted souls relishing the respite from the toil of everyday living. None of them had moved for hours, not even unconsciously into a more comfortable position. Their utter stillness and worn-out covers reflected a stark, almost sickly need for night to extend beyond the arbitrary border of day. Their motionless figures in the hollow silence of the basement begged darkness to continue, the snow to keep on dusting the bowels of the city, and the stars to go on shining for the weary of spirit.

The telephone rang, disrupting the regularity of their breathing. Apollinaire groped for the receiver, but the baby had already started to cry. Adèle reared up like a snake about to bite and swore in her mother tongue. Scrambling out of bed, she went to soothe the child, who was in the little room next to their own. She moved through the darkness, tall and sturdy, without any fear of obstacles. The *pagne* she was wearing accentuated the arch of her back

"Hello?"

"Schweitzer? Get over here, it's urgent!"

"Nicéphore, I was sleeping! Can't it wait till morning?"

"No, Doctor."

Apollinaire, called Schweitzer by his countrymen, understood that Nicéphore needed medical help.

"All right, I'm on my way," he said, his voice still groggy from the intrusion.

Apollinaire sprang out of bed and realized that Anne had stopped crying. He could hear her sucking at her mother's breast.

"Where are you going now?" Adèle's tone was more listless than annoyed.

"It's an e-m-mergency," he stammered.

He slipped on his khaki pants, white shirt and black sweater, snatched his coat off the hook, and zigzagged through the toys scattered outside the baby's room. After running a damp wash-cloth over his face, he grabbed his medical bag. The scratches here and there in the leather betrayed its age. The metal clasp was gone; only a black shoelace prevented the contents from falling out.

"I'll call you if I'm held up."

"No. I don't want you to wake the baby. I know you're going to see that lunatic Nicéphore. If I need you, *I'll* call you."

Apollinaire didn't answer. He left the apartment through the narrow door, which he quickly closed and locked behind him. The ice-covered stairs led up to a small walkway between the two houses. He climbed the steps carefully, having fallen many times. His landlord, Kevin Watson, was a reserved man, a loner, a penny-pincher. As usual, he had turned off all the outside lights.

ON THE DRIVE over, Apollinaire thought about Adèle. She had a certain resignation about her which lingered, even after a good night's sleep. He guessed she was fed up with living on the verge of poverty. Her disappointment had taken hold, like a virus in a healthy body. These past five winters in Canada hadn't been easy. The couple was having a hard time making ends meet. Adèle was working as a cleaning lady at a downtown hotel. He was employed as a call centre agent for a telephone company, but he frequently changed jobs. He had been with a travel agency and a pizzeria, not to mention a delivery company. In Africa, he had been a physician. In Canada, he didn't have a licence to practise.

A passerby hailed his cab near a traffic light. The doctor drove on without even turning his head. Deep in thought, he had forgotten to switch off the top lamp. Nicéphore's place was ten minutes away, in a densely populated neighbourhood in the west end. Seedy bars lined the street like a string of cheap pearls. Neon signs were still lit in an attempt to brighten up the atmosphere, but to no avail. Their dim halos were swallowed up by the whiteness of the empty streets and sidewalks. Apollinaire parked close to Lansdowne, entered Nicéphore's building through the dilapidated front door, and strode up the stairs. He knocked once, and Nicéphore's wife Marcella appeared, her two little boys clinging to her hips.

"He's in the bedroom," she said, turning and walking away.

Apollinaire found Nicéphore in bed with a drenched bandage around his neck.

"Ouff, Brother. I'm hurtin' here," croaked Nicéphore.

The dressing, soaked with blood and Mercurochrome, was about to fall off. The doctor opened his bag, slipped on a pair of latex gloves, and removed it without a word. The cut, which was wide but shallow, hadn't stopped bleeding. Apollinaire examined it more closely to assess the damage. He touched the skin around it, and Nicéphore jumped, wincing with pain. Apollinaire asked

3

Marcella, who was waiting in the doorway, for a plastic bag. He put the saturated bandage in the bag, then disinfected the wound. When the bleeding finally stopped, he placed a fresh, wide dressing over the cut.

"There you go. It should heal on its own now. If it starts bleeding again, call me. I'll come and stitch it. You can take these pills for the pain."

Apollinaire stood up and closed his bag. "Get lots of rest. I'll come back and see you."

Nicéphore managed a faint smile of gratitude. "Schweitzer, you've saved my skin, you have no idea."

"Oh, cut the bull!" snapped Marcella, looking furious. "You only called him because I told you to."

"You, shut up! Was I talking to you?"

The twins looked on, peeking out from behind their mother's skirt. Their round black eyes took in every move their parents made. Marcella shook her head, exasperated, then turned to Apollinaire.

"He got into a fight with that stupid friend of his, Wilson, the drunk. That's how he got hurt."

"Get out of here!" yelled Nicéphore.

Apollinaire gestured for them to calm down. "Marcella, go put the boys to bed. It's late. I want to speak to your husband."

She grunted and left the room, the twins following right behind her. The doctor set his bag down by the bed and began pacing back and forth wordlessly. He was a tall man with a slight paunch, revealing a lack of exercise. His grey-flecked hair, angular face and searching eyes made people pay attention to him.

Apollinaire was barely forty, but moved like someone twice his age.

"Tell me."

"Tell you what?"

"How you got hurt."

Nicéphore acted as if he wanted to change positions in bed, to buy some time to think. "Is it serious?"

"You're lucky. He missed your jugular."

An icy silence followed. Nicéphore scratched his head. His bare torso, smooth and lean, glistened under the pale ceiling light.

"Marcella's right. It was Wilson. But it was an accident! He didn't really mean to. We'd had a few beers in that rat hole on Dundas." Nicéphore stopped abruptly. "You know Wilson?"

"Vaguely. He's the guy from Nova Scotia, right?"

"Yeah, that's him. We were horsing around as usual."

"And?"

"That idiot, Marcella. She can't keep her mouth shut for one minute."

"I would've asked you what happened anyway."

This was not true. Apollinaire was trying to defend Marcella. He preferred not to get involved in Nicéphore's affairs. The man was too violent. And how could he help him? Certainly not by going to the police. Treating someone when you don't have a medical licence is a serious offence.

"Go on. Then what happened? I'm waiting."

Nicéphore looked at the doctor's stern face. He didn't like the man much. He suspected Apollinaire was after his wife. And there were quite the rumours about him—that his hands were "unclean," that he had collaborated with the bloody dictatorship back in Africa. Nicéphore didn't feel he was in danger, but he thought he had better cooperate in case the rumours were true.

"I don't know. I think I owe him some money or something. We'd had a few beers."

"Was he the one who pulled the knife?"

"Yeah. A long, sharp thing. I didn't see it coming. I was on the floor in two seconds, bleeding. And Wilson had vanished. I wasn't goin' wait around for the cops!"

"You should've."

"Don't lecture me. Look, Wilson's a friend. Besides, it's too late. If I go to the cops now, they'll ask me who fixed me up."

"You want to shut me up, eh?" The doctor hadn't appreciated that last comment. "Let me give you some friendly advice. Don't go shooting your mouth off when you're drunk."

Nicéphore didn't reply. He closed his eyes as if wanting to sleep. Apollinaire left the room and found Marcella in the kitchen.

"Here, this is for your family," she said, handing the doctor a plastic bag containing a huge frozen chicken. He politely declined. He never accepted anything. He didn't treat people for gain; he did it out of necessity. He still needed to feel like a doctor. After all, it was his profession. Without it, he was nothing. Nobody.

Marcella gave Apollinaire a conspiratorial look. "Meet me behind the building. I have to talk to you."

He nodded.

Apollinaire waited by the trash bins, shivering. Although he was wearing gloves, his fingers stung from the cold. He exhaled deeply, his vaporous breath dissipating into the night air. He knew what Marcella wanted to talk to him about: Nicéphore and how he treated her. He turned up his collar and stamped his foot, the smell of garbage becoming unbearable. Marcella finally appeared carrying two bags of waste. The brown coat she was wearing must have been her husband's because it hung so loosely. She tossed the bags into the bin and walked over to him.

"I'm afraid. He's started again."

"Hitting you, you mean?"

"Yes."

Her lips were quivering. Apollinaire wondered if it was the cold or fear.

"He comes home drunk every night and insults me in front of the children. You have to help me—I don't know what to do anymore."

The doctor clenched his jaw in frustration and dug his hands into his pant pockets. Marcella brushed the tears from her cheeks.

"What about his promise?" he asked, referring to the anger management sessions Nicéphore had agreed to take.

"He hasn't been going for the last week. He says he's looking for work. What a joke! He's just been drinking away the money I give him."

"The money *you* give him?"

"Yes, and if I don't, he flies into a rage."

"I'll speak to him."

"Not when he's still drunk. There's no point." Marcella shivered under her coat. "Talk to him once he's slept it off. But don't tell him we spoke. He'd be insanely jealous."

"Don't worry, he won't find out. Go back in now, otherwise he'll be suspicious."

He watched the young woman disappear into the darkness, sensing the defeat in her fragile figure. He had met Marcella in Canada a few years earlier. She wasn't a close friend, but he felt obliged to help her. They were from the same village, the same world, and that meant everything to a woman like Marcella. Apollinaire knew it and tried not to disappoint her. He saw her struggling with a violent husband in a cold country, but he didn't have the heart to tell her there was nothing he could do. Marcella had chosen him as her confidant, her lifeline. He could see the loneliness in the premature lines on her face, and he had to look down every time he felt the urge to brush her off. This woman, whom he glanced at furtively now and then, was like a lost child in a schoolyard governed by rules she didn't know. Marcella saw Apollinaire as a witness to her life, someone who could testify to where she was from, someone who knew that her life in the tropics had not been a mirage.

II

Taxi in the Night

THE TAXI, A recent Ford model, did not belong to Apollinaire. His friend, Philibert N'Zumba, had lent it to him while he was away in the United States getting married. Philibert had managed to buy his owner's licence after driving a cab for two decades; now he was his own boss. At fifty, he had finally saved a little money and his next step was to find a wife, the dowry no longer being a problem. Philibert wrote to an old friend who had recently settled in Arizona and had a daughter just twenty. He exchanged a few letters with her, gathered she was willing and, with her father's consent, went down to propose. That's how Apollinaire ended up with the taxi for a few days.

The car barely made a sound beyond a low purr. Apollinaire was driving home now and wanted to break the unsettling silence. He grabbed the first cassette he could find and slipped it into the player.

"Taxi!"

After a brief hesitation, he decided to stop. He thought the company would do him good. A young man in his twenties, with blond hair and blue eyes, opened the door, his frosty breath circling his angelic head as he hopped into the back seat.

"What a winter," said the young man, rubbing his hands.

"Yeah, it's a real deep-freeze out there. Where are you going?"

"To Forest Hill."

Apollinaire headed for one of the poshest neighbourhoods in the city. His passenger smelled of tobacco. The mere presence of another soul was comforting. He regained a sense of peace, no longer feeling the loneliness that had been tightening his throat. What's more, he now had a destination that was not the hovel he lived in.

"What's the music?"

"Oh, I'm sorry. Is it too loud?"

"No, it's fine. I've just come from a going-away party for a colleague who's moving to New York. Trust me, the music there was louder than this. It's nice," added the young man after a moment's pause. "Is it African?"

"Yes." Apollinaire answered tersely, not wanting to get into a conversation. But his curiosity got the better of him. "I don't suppose you've ever been to Africa?"

"No. The only warm place I've been to is Dominica. I wouldn't mind going back, with the frigid weather we're having here."

The car pulled up at one of the stately homes. The passenger cut the conversation short and gave the driver a generous tip.

Apollinaire decided to drive slowly to admire the houses. He stopped in front of some of them. At dawn, they were even more magnificent than in daytime. Encased in outside lights, they looked like timeless jewels. The rooftops—arched, sloping and even circular—were surrounded by majestic white conifers that cast evanescent shadows. The stone walls of many homes were covered with dormant ivy. The windows lit from within gleamed like the eyes of a feline stalking prey. Apollinaire drove on and pulled over again, resting his gaze on the snowy lawns and flagstones barely visible beneath the ivory mantle. Some yards had an empty kennel, others a vacant set of swings. Not all the luxury cars had been sheltered from the snowfall. The ones left out in driveways were hardly recognizable under the fresh blanket. Apollinaire was in no hurry to get back to his postage-stamp apartment. He closed his eyes and let his mind go blank, listening intently to the silence around him. The tick-tock of his turn signal eventually caught his attention. He found it soothing. The sound was steady, ordinary, mandatory. Something he could count on. He decided to slip in another cassette.

III

Fela Anikulapo Kuti

APOLLINAIRE HAD BEEN listening to the music for some time when the sun rose. He was now hurrying to get home. He had to take over for Adèle, who would be leaving for work. He drove through the city, which was starting to bustle, the traffic growing thicker. People ran to catch streetcars that refused to wait for them. Some shook their fists in the air and glared at the drivers pulling away. The entire scene was becoming hectic and chaotic. Some pedestrians tried to hail him, but in vain. Others even banged their briefcases on his windshield to get him to stop. Apollinaire saw them as deranged puppets. The strings of their tightly constructed schedules had come unravelled, and their passivity had given way to anger bordering on hysteria. He found it all so absurd: going to such lengths to be trapped in an anthill for eight hours. He turned up the music to shut out the vibrations of the raging city.

The doctor was listening to Fela Anikulapo Kuti, the king of Afrobeat. Born in Nigeria, Fela was a short, thin, unconventional artist—a polygamist who liked to play saxophone scantily clad. His music didn't feature guitars like that of many central African bands, but emphasized wind instruments and electric keyboards.

Fela challenged the political establishment his entire life, heaping scorn on the power-hungry military pawns in his country. This repeatedly landed him in prison. Called the Black President by his sympathizers, he sang in Africanized pidgin English. Often victimized by thug soldiers, Fela reminded Apollinaire that he was from a violent, even cruel continent.

In this wintry world, Fela's voice seemed to come from another universe. The song, *Yellow Fever*, criticized Africans bent on using skin-lightening creams, ridiculing those discoloured by the cheap cosmetics. Apollinaire bobbed his head to the music. In his homeland, they were called "fantas," after the orange-flavoured soft drink. They stood out amid the dark-skinned population. The doctor remembered women hawkers with sallow faces but black fingers. Their natural pigment had remained in some spots, the folds of their knuckles and elbows providing a refuge from the harsh products. Some local soccer stars, unable to hide their knees during games, gave spectators a good laugh as well as a show of their athletic prowess. Fantas were also called "ambitious" because they lightened their bodies to be beautiful. They wanted to be admired by the multitude of poor and often destitute blacks. But these products could be dangerous. Apollinaire, who had now reached his apartment, recalled a heartbreaking case. The patient was barely thirty. She was ambitious all right. She had used so much bleaching cream that her cheeks had turned almost pink and her skin, translucent from head to toe. After her operation for acute appendicitis, Apollinaire couldn't stitch her. Every time he tried, her skin tore. He murmured the cause of death: "acute peritonitis, internal bleeding and infection." Ambition in Africa was sometimes fatal.

IV

A Turbulent Morning

"YOU'RE GOING to make me late one of these days."

Adèle held out the baby to her husband. Apollinaire took Anne into his arms and kissed her on the forehead. His wife disappeared into the cramped bathroom to finish getting ready for work. Anne was almost two, her eyes alert and inquisitive, her skin dark, her kinky black hair styled in an Afro. She put her hands on her father's face. Adèle returned to the living room and walked past Apollinaire, frowning. The hotel where she worked was in the downtown core; her shift started early in the morning and ended in the afternoon. She drew her braids up into a bun and fit her sneakers into a black bag—going from floor to floor cleaning rooms required comfortable footwear.

"Her food for the day's in the fridge. Just heat it up."

"Okay. Say goodbye to Mama, Anne."

The little girl looked as if she wanted to cry.

"Her name's Nyngone, not Anne," replied Adèle, irked.

"She has both first names."

"Yes, but it's better to call her by her African name."

"Why?"

Adèle went to put on her coat. "The women I work with call their children Jibril, Chaka, and who knows what else. They even come up with names like Shabu and Shayina. We're African and we baptize our baby *Anne*. It's backwards!"

Adèle pulled on her brown leather boots, looking at her husband to see his reaction.

"There are Catholic names in both our families," said Apollinaire.

"There aren't just Catholics back home. There are Muslims, Protestants, Jehovah Witnesses, Animists . . . There's everything."

"I know, but we were baptized Catholic. It's not our fault if we were colonized by the French."

"Being Catholic doesn't mean anything. You don't seem to understand that it's just a way of brainwashing people. We're African before we're Catholic."

Adèle's irritation upset Anne, who tensed up in her father's arms.

"The French call their children Pierre and Jean. The English, James and Mary. Why does my daughter have to be called Anne?"

The little girl burst out crying, and Apollinaire clasped her gently in his arms. Adèle left the apartment, slamming the door. She returned a few minutes later, having forgotten her bus tokens. Before she departed again, she said, "I don't have food in my stomach because I'm Catholic. I have food in my stomach because I work. Being Catholic doesn't do much for me. It's my hands that enable me to put food on the table."

Apollinaire didn't reply. He just rocked Anne, who was still fussing. He didn't think Adèle's reaction had anything to do with the baby's name. It had more to do with failure. His failure. Him. The doctor, certain to rise in his career, yet still eking out a living. Was it about him or her? He wasn't sure anymore. Adèle had studied in Africa, too, training to be a nurse. Apollinaire bit his lip. He no longer knew what to think. A feeling of uncertainty had

14

grown between him and his wife. He could no longer clearly discern if what she said was what she thought. Everything was becoming hazy, as if a strange poison was seeping into their relationship, their life together. Was it really even a life?

He switched on the television and tried to console himself by watching news about people who were less fortunate, people who had lost their homes in a bombing and had nothing to eat. The newscaster seemed unmoved. He wore the solemn expression of a professional who knows the routine. But the images of starving people did not console him. There's something about injustice that other injustices cannot relieve; a tear of blood among the cracks in the heart that never congeals. Apollinaire sat his daughter down on the rug and placed a few toys around her. She stood up, clutching his pant leg.

All of a sudden, he felt utterly exhausted. He didn't have time to sleep: he had to take care of Anne. He shook his head thinking about what his friends in Africa would say. No one would believe him if he told them that he changed his daughter's diapers. It was shameful for a man to perform such chores. Especially a doctor, who should have the means to hire domestic help. He could never mention that he washed the dishes. None of his former colleagues would ever be able to imagine him plunging his hands into a sinkful of soapy water. Where on earth was his wife? If he didn't have a domestic, a man could at least count on his wife.

Once he had changed Anne and put the dishes away, he decided to tell her a story, to put her to sleep. He knew she wasn't tired; still, he hoped to have a couple of hours to himself by putting her down. Of course she wouldn't understand the tale, but he knew that the tone of his voice would be enough to lull her. Apollinaire sat with his daughter nestled in his arms, her head resting on his shoulder. Tension rose in his throat as he recalled the first time he heard the story. He was fourteen and had just gone to live with his uncle in the capital of his homeland. When he heard

15

Pierre Akendengue's voice over his uncle's transistor radio, it was as if the musician-storyteller was right there beside him. He felt sad because he had just left his family and his village. Thanks to his grades, his father had chosen him over his five siblings to attend school in the city.

"There was a young man named Poé," began Apollinaire, "who made it rain as soon as he started to sing. Poé left for the big city, because his ill-fated ability had angered the villagers. He met some leopard men and an owl woman along the way. Then he took a pirogue and sailed into the city on a market day. There he heard the women hawkers shout, 'Gifts a plenty!' to let people know that the prices were so very low. Poé saw some children marching as one and declared, 'All religion serves a regime.' People heard his words and threw him in prison, but he started to sing and the rain came pouring down. The jail keeper, fearing a flood, decided to release him and ordered him to leave the country. Poé went to seek his fortune elsewhere, living abroad like a legionnaire. Sometimes he made drops of rain fall, sometimes drops of blood, sometimes drops mixed with the blood of innocents. Poé wanted to return home, because he felt it was unworthy to be living without giving to the liberation of his motherland."

Apollinaire stopped the story because his little girl had fallen asleep. He took care not to hold her too tightly. He remembered the end of the tale, an enigmatic smile appearing on his face. Once back home, Poé committed an act for which he was sentenced to hang. As he was about to be executed, he sang once more. This time, he disappeared amid the flood, never to be seen again. That's why a bird can be heard singing "Poé! Poé! Poé!" in the Land of Africa. The story had fascinated Apollinaire when he was young and had just left home. He thought that Pierre Akendengue was talking about him, about his fate. People in his village had shown him leopard men and told him they fed on blood. He had seen the owl woman in the story; she came out solely at night and walked mournfully about. He had to be Poé because he, too, longed for freedom. The capital was half a world away, but he would return home one day to his people. He would return, the prodigal son, with his skills enriched, and his mother tongue speckled with French from France. He would speak of freedom for the toil-worn farmers who were his mother and father.

Apollinaire started work at noon. He still had time to lie down and try to recuperate before he had to leave. His chance of resting disappeared when the telephone rang.

"Schweitzer?"

"Philibert!"

It was the owner of the taxi he was driving.

"You've got nothing better to do than to call me when you're about to get married?"

Philibert broke into laughter. "She's beautiful, Schweitzer!"

"You'd better be careful someone doesn't steal her from you." Apollinaire was teasing his friend even though he had advised him against marrying her. A traditional wedding, the dowry and all the ceremony for a woman young enough to be his daughter—he wasn't marrying for love. But Philibert was stubborn. "An African in his fifties has to get married the way we do back home!" he had replied. It seemed to be a point of honour.

"How's my taxi?"

"Fine."

"I don't have much time. We're going away tomorrow, and we're getting ready now," said Philibert. "Can you send me the phone number of a guy named John Coleman? His business card's in the glovebox. I need all his contact info. Can you fax it to me as soon as possible?"

"No problem."

Philibert gave him his fax number in Arizona. Apollinaire reassured him that he'd take care of it. When he hung up, he

17

accidentally knocked down an old photo of Adèle in high school. Memories flashed through his mind as he sat by the phone contemplating the young woman of nineteen with the dazzling smile. The photo had yellowed and the edges were worn, but the image of Adèle showed an exuberance. A joyfulness now faded. They had met in high school, in their last year before university. He remembered the first time he saw her. That day, the sun had reached its zenith, and the stream of students leaving the school looked like a column of ants drawn by an enticing scent. Adèle was wearing a bag across her shoulder. More slender than most of the girls, she was walking up the hill to the Deux Palmiers, chatting with her friends. Her graceful curves and slightly lustrous skin in the sunlight exuded sensuality. Apollinaire, behind her, was heading in the same direction but turning off well before her: the Deux Palmiers was for the middle class. He eyed her so intently that, from then on, he could recognize her from afar.

Not the endless student chatter, squealing brakes, honking horns or stifling heat ever distracted him from watching her. Adèle finally noticed him, although he avoided meeting her gaze. Occasionally, she would go to Apollinaire's neighbourhood after school. He lived in a working-class district, which the French colonists had called the Camp. They had ordered their domestics to live close by their residential area; that was where Adèle lived.

With time, long after the country became independent, drinking spots and greasy spoons opened up and thrived in the Camp. The bars on both sides of the main street attempted to draw customers by turning up their music. Students went to those places to dance and unwind. Sometimes they bumped into a monitor from their school having a drink. There was a tacit agreement between them—the Camp was neutral territory. The monitor would consume his beer while the students writhed to the music of their favourite bands. Sometimes they even raised a glass to one another. However, students could not run into a monitor along the wall separating the school from the Camp. If they were caught scaling the Berlin Wall, as they called it, the monitor would become stern-faced and order them to report to his office. Most of the students knew what that meant: spending the weekend cleaning the school washrooms or sponging down the principal's car.

It was at a bar with a tin roof that Apollinaire finally spoke to the young woman who so attracted him. They exchanged their first words amidst a bunch of hip-swaying students, surrounded by the usual drunkards, heat-dazed monitors, and a few whites who had ventured into the strange-looking crowd sweating from head to toe. No waitresses. Customers ordered at the counter.

The students would choose their hangout, pinball machine or soccer table. They enjoyed themselves to the music of Franco, Rochereau, Abeti and M'pongo Love—all popular singers capable of transforming a group of shy young students into experts at spectacular hip gyrations. The music played over rundown loudspeakers, the percussion shaking the foundations of those rickety structures. Despite the ambient cacophony, patrons were always able to flaunt their best dance moves.

Adèle would go to M'as-tu vu?, her favourite bar, to dance with her friends. It was one of the most decrepit dives in the area. Alcohol vapours hung so thickly in the air that they seemed to have permeated the wobbly little tables and chairs. Apollinaire knew Adèle liked that place. Although she didn't have any male friends, she and her girlfriends were known for choosing the seediest clubs for dancing. They would frequent those bars for close encounters with scum. The challenge was never to let themselves be lured by a low-life. The young men who patronized M'as-tu vu? were incorrigible pick-up artists—snake charmers with a feverish gaze and slicked-back hair. They would circle the young women, weaving among them like famished sharks, predators who knew how to wait until just the right moment to

19

pounce on their prey. They certainly dressed for it, wearing slacks with knife-edge creases and open-collar shirts showing off chest hair. They always mastered the trendiest dance steps, rolling their hips and buttocks with such vigour that they drew excited squeals of admiration from some of the girls. With bold moves and electrifying pelvic rotations, they would go up to Adèle and some of the other young women, miming the act of love-making. But they would never touch them. Like hummingbirds hovering around flowers, they would flap their limbs so nimbly that no one could distinguish their quick steps.

The students would form a circle and each one would take a turn in the centre, to showcase his or her talents. Apollinaire remembered the time that Adèle moved into the middle and took his breath away. Her grace and fluidity were like those of a tightrope walker at the height of her glory. She rolled her hips confidently but not lasciviously, varying her steps while keeping time. Her legs, waist and spine all seemed to obey different commands. When she left the centre, she feigned the serenity of a dancer able to tame the demon in her. But Apollinaire noticed the sparkle in her eyes, the straightness of her torso pushing out her breasts, and the energetic arch of her back.

One day when she was leaving the entrancing circle, Apollinaire went up to her, using the final exams as an excuse to speak to her. She responded amicably. He knew he had to put his best foot forward. He had a reputation as a hard worker. A couple of months before the university entrance exams, his help would surely be welcome. He had no trouble convincing her that they should study together. For a number of months, nothing special happened. Adèle was someone who didn't reveal much about herself. Apollinaire was too afraid of making a mistake to take any initiative. It took him a full year to win her over.

He didn't attach much importance to style. Some women would have never held that against him, but Adèle admired elegance in men. That said, his attractive physique and self-assured bearing made up for his lack of taste in clothing and his tendency to be taciturn, out of modesty. Apollinaire thought he had become reserved after leaving his village to live at his uncle's house in the city. What an austere home it happened to be, the head of the family widowed and sullen. His uncle, a bus driver, kept his teeth clenched most of the time. He spoke only to say grace before meals, issue orders to his seven children, and tell them when he expected to be home. Fortunately for Apollinaire, he was not mean. His uncle was deeply bitter though, like many people who question God's purpose in leaving them wifeless with a large family.

Apollinaire still wondered how Adèle, the daughter of a chauffeur-driven government official, could have fallen for him, the son of a farmer who could barely read. Not only that, he had the misfortune of being a poor dancer, when a man's agility on the dance floor was his trump card in African courtship. Despite these drawbacks, Apollinaire had the advantage of being able to explain the most complex academic questions with disconcerting simplicity. His unassuming nature and melodious voice earned him growing respect from his friends as well as Adèle. His rivals could show off if they liked, spritzing themselves with Givenchy and wearing the latest styles, but they couldn't eclipse him. He finally managed to capture Adèle's heart once and for all.

V

Fatima and Kevin Watson

THE DOORBELL RANG twice in rapid succession. It was Fatima, Anne's babysitter. A big black woman in her thirties, winded by even the shortest walk. She spoke to Anne first.

"Hi Darlin'. I'm here."

The doctor felt relieved that she had finally arrived. He didn't want to be late for work. He smiled at her and handed her the baby, who had just awoken.

"Her food's ready to go. All you have to do is heat it up. And there's some chicken and vegetables in the fridge for your lunch."

Apollinaire went into the bedroom to change. When he came back out, Fatima cleared her throat to attract his attention.

"Doctor?"

"Yes?"

Apollinaire wasn't used to being called Doctor anymore. Every time someone addressed him by that title, he felt as if he was breaking the law.

"I have a little problem."

The doctor was always amused by how awkward Africans seemed when they spoke to a physician, regardless of their ailment.

They invariably had a look of deference, as if their condition—like that of so many others—was a matter of life or death.

"It's my foot. My toes are hurting me."

Fatima removed her shoe and showed Apollinaire her corns.

He knew what she wanted: free medication. He didn't make her ask for it.

"Just a minute."

He went to rummage through his medical bag. A few moments later, he returned looking triumphant.

"This is the last antiseptic ointment I have. You don't need to use much. I also want you to soak your foot in salt water. And stop wearing those," he said, pointing to her high heels. "I know you have to look good, but those shoes are hurting your toes."

"Okay."

After getting cleaned up, Apollinaire left the apartment. He had about thirty minutes before he had to start work. As he was stepping into the cab, he heard someone call him.

"Apolli!"

It was his landlord. Only Kevin Watson could have come up with such an unpleasant diminutive. Apollinaire furrowed his brow, irritated by the abbreviation of his name.

In walking toward Watson, the doctor noticed that the man had dressed with care. He was wearing black slacks, a brown shirt and a light red wool sweater under a long grey coat that looked somewhat light for winter. As Apollinaire approached the house, he realized that he felt cold. The snow had melted in a few hours, but the wind stung his ears and chapped his lips. He buttoned his coat up to the collar as he neared the steps. His landlord stood motionless in front of the half-open door. Greying and beginning to bald, he was short, pale, and wore a rather untidy chinstrap beard.

He hardly moved his penetrating gaze from Apollinaire. The doctor often wondered if his landlord was trying to read him, to break the conventional barrier between them. Watson looked like a Jansenist who had strayed into the wrong age: his solemn attire and balding pate contributed to his image as a diehard clergyman. He signalled to Apollinaire to follow him, revealing in the dim hallway the bare, almost white spot at his crown, his pope's skullcap.

"I have something to show you. I hope you have a little time."

Apollinaire nodded. He was a ten-minute drive from work. The two men walked into the living room. It, too, was sombre, the closed curtains letting in a sole persistent ray of light. Apollinaire's eyes had to adjust to the darkness before he could move about. A grand piano stood silent by the leather couch and chairs. The doctor had never heard it in the basement. Atop the instrument sat a black and white photo of Watson on a beach. He would have been twenty at most. The young man he was looked to be revelling in life's bounty back then. A bygone time, a distant time. Watson had never invited Apollinaire into his home. In fact, he liked his solitude. The doctor assumed he was widowed, but Adèle thought he must be divorced. The retired real estate agent never talked about himself.

Watson picked up the newspaper lying on the couch and held it out to the doctor. It was the neighbourhood gazette.

"Read page three," he said, his eyes sparkling with excitement.

The Sentinel had printed a long article about Apollinaire, written by Watson. To the right of the text appeared the doctor's photo. An ID photo. In the article, the landlord explained that he was acquainted with an immigrant who wanted nothing more than to fit into Canadian society but felt shut out. Apollinaire was a physician. However, our system of assessing foreign-trained doctors prevented worthy people like him from practising their professions. In two years, Apollinaire had passed two difficult exams prepared by the medical regulatory authorities, while working to keep a roof over his head. He still had to take other

24

exams, some clinical, some general. These requirements did not consider the calibre of training of certain practitioners, who were reduced to selling pizza. The article pointed out the glaring shortage of physicians in this country. It called for an in-depth reform of the system, to meet the needs of the many Canadians waiting for a doctor to relieve them of their suffering.

Apollinaire folded the newspaper slowly and smiled out of politeness.

"It's very good. Thanks for writing it."

"Oh, it's nothing," replied Watson, acting offended by the gratitude. "All I did was tell the truth. Your situation's unacceptable."

Apollinaire remained silent.

"Don't worry. I have influential friends in Ottawa. This has to change, but you'll need to be patient," said Watson, adding, "I support you completely."

Apollinaire's smile turned into something of a grimace. He didn't like people telling him he needed to be patient, to wait. Time didn't wait. He controlled his voice and body language; Watson didn't suspect he was angry. He had learned long ago to avoid reacting to right-thinking people, hypocrites with well-lined pockets who liked to talk to him about patience and perseverance. The same people who took their vacations every summer with the regularity of Swiss watches. The people who pitied "unlucky" immigrants. As if luck had anything to do with the fact that they couldn't practise their professions. The doctor narrowed his eyes slightly, but Watson didn't notice a thing. Apollinaire thought about the nights he had spent scribbling pages of notes, studying for exams that hadn't restored his status, but only kept him in poverty. His successes had been useless. Other exams had become mandatory because the regulations had changed. Adèle had often slept with the light on so that he could study. She had even paid the rent on her own so that he didn't have to work overtime. All that for an article in the local newspaper, he thought. Watson went so far as to defend him against the indifference of the masses. But wasn't Watson one of them? One of those people too busy with daily life to be interested in the fate of those from elsewhere? Why did he act as if he understood? In any event, it was too late. Apollinaire felt as if he was in a deceiving country, not a receiving country. He had at least hoped to obtain a scholarship for the last exams in light of his grades on the first ones. He had been sure he would be granted his licence. He and Adèle had conceived Anne in the hope of starting anew. With the initial exams behind him and the child born, they thought they were on the doorstep to happy days. But, in the end, the baby came into a world of bitterness, because after the exams came other assessments. They loved Anne with all their hearts, but there were times when they had difficulty concealing the disappointment that accompanied her birth.

"Could I have some water? My throat's dry."

Watson hurried into the kitchen and returned with a glass. He handed it to Apollinaire, looking concerned. "It's probably fatigue," he concluded.

Apollinaire emptied the glass in one go and remembered that he had to leave for work. As he was walking out, he tripped over a stack of newspapers on the floor, inwardly cursing the lack of light in the house. Watson told him to ignore the scattered pages, but he felt obliged to straighten them up. He noticed an X-ray that had fallen out of the pile. The two men exchanged an awkward glance. Apollinaire tidied up the sheets and, as he was descending the front steps to the sidewalk, Watson stopped him by laying his hand on his shoulder.

"You forgot this," he said, holding out the newspaper to Apollinaire. "Wait a minute," he added. He went back inside, bent down and riffled through the stack of papers on the floor. Then he stood back up, the X-ray in hand, and slipped it into Apollinaire's copy of *The Sentinel*, making sure the doctor had seen it.

"Enjoy the film," he said.
Puzzled, the doctor nodded as he left.

VI

Servants from Elsewhere

APOLLINAIRE WORKED AT a call centre, owned by a private telephone company, in a huge bustling room where employees attended the phones day and night. His job was to answer questions from consumers seeking low rates, and to calm down customers dissatisfied with their service. Every day, he spoke to strangers on the line. That day, some of the employees were scanning their computer screens; others were taking notes. They all had to wear headsets and to answer queries as quickly and thoroughly as possible. Although the volume of calls was too high, the supervisors required attendants to provide a full explanation of the special offers. The company insisted on courtesy: customers were right even when they were wrong.

Apollinaire entered the room on the fifteenth floor of the bland building, taking a deep breath as if preparing to dive under water and into a world full of danger. His colleagues, sitting side by side, looked busy. They were all speaking at the same time, their jumbled voices creating a low-pitched din. The repetitive conversations no longer bothered them. They didn't raise their tone, but addressed callers with the persistence of door-to-door salespeople. They also muttered under their breath; only a keen ear could decipher their homicidal grumblings. Although the telephones didn't sound, a thousand rings would have never irritated Apollinaire as much as the constant profanities of his co-workers. They readily switched from cursing to kowtowing. From rage to submission. Submission for a bi-monthly paycheque. He remembered his first day on the job and how disgusted he had felt. He had seen the fear on their faces, as they worried about being dismissed for vague economic reasons. They often whispered or talked about things other than the routine work. All the phones were monitored. Officially, the company listened in, to ensure that employees were doing their jobs. In reality, it wanted employees to be aware that they were being supervised at all times. Attendants often lifted their eyes to the board in the corner of the long room. In red appeared the names of those with poor or average performance; in black, the stars of speed and accuracy on the phone. They outshone the others because they were better at enrolling new customers, winning back those who had switched companies, and placating the quarrelsome. Apollinaire seemed to check his brain at the door every day when he got to the office. He had to follow orders and answer mindless questions, which callers showered on him like acid rain.

He greeted Marguerita, the attendance clerk, as he headed toward his workstation.

"How are you?"

"Fine, when you're on time."

The doctor smiled at her, then signed the attendance sheet.

"A lot of calls today?"

"Yes. More than usual. The company ran ads out west, so watch what you say," she warned, raising her index finger like a school teacher. "You know the rule."

"You can count on me."

She frowned as if he had not taken her seriously. Marguerita was in her fifties, heavily made up and verging on obese. She was quite likeable, with her Aztec grandmother looks, full cheeks and double chin.

"Thanks for warning me."

This last comment seemed to put her at ease. Apollinaire knew the rules in this case. Attendants were not to talk about the weather. People, especially in the western part of the country, could take offence if it was snowing there and sunny in Toronto. Another rule: never let them know they were calling Toronto. Consumers had difficulty understanding why they had to call a centre thousands of kilometres away simply to subscribe to a telephone service. It meant lost jobs for their region. Greedy Toronto didn't need yet another office.

"Schweitzer! Where have you been these past few days?"

"What do mean, Abdoulaye? I'm here every day!"

"I mean after work."

Apollinaire shook his co-worker's hand. Africans liked to do that.

"Yeah, I know. I've been busy with the family," explained the doctor, putting on his headset.

"I know what that's like. Don't forget, I have five kids. Two here and three back home."

The doctor was going to ask him how things were in Senegal, when Abdoulaye straightened up in his chair.

"Abdoulaye Diallo. How may I help you?"

Apollinaire dropped the conversation and connected his headset. He took out a pen and some paper so he could jot down complicated customer names before keying them into his computer. He pulled a pink booklet out of his pants pocket. It was the customer conversation guide. The doctor no longer referred to it: he knew it by heart. However, he kept it close at hand in case an overzealous supervisor walked down his aisle. Those people were a separate breed—the illegitimate offspring of the devil incarnate. They had the power to help you or to burden you with work befitting galley slaves. Their vicious criticism, like overseers' lashes, would shred your morale. Even their gaze sometimes evoked the cruelty of slave drivers in the cane fields. They hardly ever smiled except when they found fault with one of their whipping boys. The supervisors were hand-picked. Most would have sold their mother to get ahead. They were recruited young so they could be moulded into devout supporters of the employer's cause. They listened in on customer calls and chided attendants for their handling of them. They made a point of informing employees when their co-workers left the company permanently. They never forgot a worker's birthday, and used the opportunity to ingratiate themselves with those unaware of their ploys. Never had Apollinaire heard one of them speak of "dismissal." They were always "unfortunate voluntary separations." With their cold smiles, they reminded him of morticians. The doctor was convinced that there was nothing good, natural or warm about them. Their constant obsession with productivity and performance had quashed their more noble feelings.

Abdoulaye carefully followed the pink guide, using it to ask callers questions. He was meticulous by nature. Apollinaire looked at him discreetly. His skin was very dark, his domed forehead accentuated by his receding hairline. He had angular features like an ebony sculpture and a deep voice with the prosody typical of a strong accent. The doctor took advantage of the brief lull between callers to listen to Abdoulaye's conversation.

"Our long distance is unlimited. You can call anywhere you like, anytime you like."

Apollinaire tried to catch his co-worker's eye. With a mocking smile, he started to repeat what he was saying in a hushed tone.

"What do you think of this unique offer?"

Abdoulaye motioned Apollinaire to stop mimicking him. The beep in the doctor's headset announced an incoming call.

"Apollinaire Mavoungou. Thank you for calling. How may I help you?

"Apolli . . . what?"

He immediately understood that he was dealing with an antagonistic customer. He often came across this type of person, whom he and Abdoulaye called "apes."

"Apollinaire Mavoungou. May I help you?"

The caller snickered, asking "Are you in Canada?"

"Yes, Ma'am," replied the doctor, annoyed. He couldn't say he was in Toronto because of the rule.

"With a name like that, you must be in Toronto."

Apollinaire let the remark go, but tensed up all the same.

"I want some information about your long-distance plans."

He knew the conversation was being monitored. Veins appeared on his temples as he tried to control the pressure in his chest. Unusual for him, he picked up the guide and started reading it off. By reciting the company's offers, he had time to calm down. And he wasn't thinking anymore. That was the thing to avoid. Thinking. Using his sense of repartee with this caller would have cost him his job. He was convinced of that. Thus, he was to be the company's best robot. He had to seal his mouth, divert the natural flow of blood in his veins, silence the drum of his rebellion, so he could go on working. Apollinaire suddenly had the impression that he was in the jungle where survival of the fittest did not mean the best. There was also survival of the most vicious. He had to wear an invisible gag, a sort of chastity belt over his face, a loathsome device that reduced him to being the subject of a corporation, a masked assailant.

"I need to ask you a few questions so I can offer you the best possible service." Apollinaire paused to swallow. "Is your telephone in your name?"

"What?"

The doctor repeated the question with patience that surprised even him.

"I can't understand a thing you're saying. Can you give me someone who speaks English?"

"But . . . I'm sure I can help you, Ma'am."

The caller could not bear Apollinaire's insistence and shouted, "I want to speak to your supervisor right now! How can this company hire people who don't even speak the language? I don't know what language you're speaking, but it isn't English!"

"Just a moment, please."

The doctor shook with anger. Standing up reflexively, he went to look for a "shark," as he called them. He came across Sébastien, a supervisor who was quite accommodating when in a good mood. Sébastien followed Apollinaire back to his workstation without hesitation. Tall and brown-haired, he looked like a ferocious dog who could be docile if rubbed the right way.

"Yes, Madam?" he asked in a professional voice.

Apollinaire stood off to the side. His co-workers, although busy, cast inquisitive glances at him. Some gave him sympathizing looks; they knew the intervention of a supervisor was not a good sign. Sébastien would make out a report, and God only knew whose hands it would end up in.

Abdoulaye caught his friend's attention between calls. "Don't worry, Brother. I've asked him to come over twice today. He's in a good mood."

"Why did *you* ask him to come over?"

"Some idiot asked me where Medicine Hat is."

Apollinaire smiled.

"Why on earth would someone name a town Medicine Hat? I told him I didn't know where the godforsaken place was. I was polite as usual, but he felt offended. He called me a dirty nigger! I think he'd been to Africa. Those people are the worst."

"Then what did you say?"

"Nothing, Brother. I have to pay the rent and feed my family."

"But how did you respond to that?"

33

"I suggested that we get back to the long-distance services I wanted to tell him about. He got all worked up and demanded to speak to a supervisor. No, in fact, he said 'I want to speak to your boss!'"

The two men sputtered with laughter.

"As if I know the name of the white guy who owns this damn company," muttered Abdoulaye, who immediately stiffened and looked robotic. He had an incoming call. "Hello, Sir."

Sébastien had just finished with Apollinaire's caller. "I want you and Abdou to come and see me before you leave today," he said. His tone was firm. His mood had changed. Apollinaire slipped his friend a note between calls, informing him that Sébastien wanted to see them. Abdoulaye rolled his eyes. From that point on, every minute seemed to crawl by, every hour to drag on. It was as if time had slowed, to punish them for their banter.

"Yes, I'm from Senegal," confirmed Abdoulaye in French to a francophone caller. "May I ask how much you spend on long distance a month? Eighty dollars on average?"

He grimaced in exasperation between questions.

"Yes, Senegal's a member of the Francophonie. You have a friend from the Ivory Coast? That's nice, Sir. Let's say eighty dollars then. With the service I'm offering you, there's no minimum number of calls abroad. Pardon? Your sister adopted a Haitian boy? That's great!"

Apollinaire glanced over occasionally to see if his friend would somehow manage to get rid of the caller. He wasn't able to follow the entire conversation: the number of calls coming in kept growing. Marguerita was right. It was a busy day.

Returning from the washroom, the doctor noticed Lynn, a fearsome shark. She worked in another department, in marketing. Lynn was training a new employee on sales techniques and had been doing so for a couple of weeks. Chrisosthome was from Burundi, a small country in central Africa. He was a highway engineer and had completed his studies in Romania. Lynn was barely out of her teens. With her blue eyes and neck-length blond hair, she looked angelic. Her face, fresh as a suckled cherub, contrasted with that of the African patriarch. She seemed even-tempered with beginners as well as experienced employees. Apollinaire wanted to continue watching her. He pretended to be looking for an important document on his table, to avoid being noticed by a supervisor. Lynn was bending down to Chrisosthome's ear, whispering the answers for him to give the caller. When the caller hung up, she put her hand on his shoulder for him to remove his earphones, then calmly explained what he should say the next time he had that type of call. Chrisosthome lifted his round eyes up to the young Scandinavian goddess, as if pleading for redemption. He apologized for his ignorance and his slowness in mastering the mechanics of telephone sales. To Apollinaire's keen eye, he had the look of a sinner on Judgment Day.

"I have to go and coach Hô and Flavio. Jacques will come and help you," she said rather loudly.

Lynn left Chrisosthome with the same smile she was wearing when she began the session. With an indifferent air, she headed over to an ageless Asian and a Mediterranean man with curly black hair. The Burundian appeared even more desperate. He knew what this meant—torture for the rest of the day. Jacques Dorion was scarcely thirty. Of average height, with short brown hair, he emanated confidence and vitality with his stiff, erect gait. He rarely smiled, except at women. With him, employees had to learn quickly. Chrisosthome had tasted Jacques's approach the previous day and didn't want to repeat the experience. Apollinaire noticed Lynn's amused expression once her back was turned to the Burundian. She had gotten rid of the lame duck without having to raise her voice. Jacques came and told Chrisosthome to take a short break; he had something to finish. He marched to his office at the end of the room, some employees acknowledging him as he passed

35

by, others looking down. For them, he was a model of success. He drove a Porsche provided by the company for his excellent work in marketing. He constantly topped the list of best salespeople for the month. Jacques had won the Employee of the Year award on several occasions. He was portly, but his natural vivacity overshadowed his plumpness. Apollinaire recalled what Chrisosthome had confided in him the day before. "Jacques's harassing me. He keeps telling me to speak louder, but I can't do that. In my culture, we're not direct. We don't shout. It's considered rude."

VII

Culture Shock

JACQUES FINALLY MADE his way back to Chrisosthome's work table and sat down beside the frantic-looking African.

"Take a few calls on your own, like a big boy, and show me what you can do. Go ahead."

Chrisosthome, head hanging, did not reply. He placed his trembling hands on the keyboard. Jacques finally pressed the button himself to activate the line. The trainee was too afraid to move. That didn't seem to bother the supervisor.

"Hello? Yes, hello, my name's Chrisosthome and . . . pardon? No. *Chrisos . . . C, H, R . . . Chriso . . .*"

Jacques signed to him to stop spelling his name. In the meantime, the caller had hung up. The supervisor disconnected the trainee's earphones, releasing a lungful of air. He ran his fingers through his hair, looking exasperated.

"What did I tell you yesterday? Speak up! People wouldn't ask you to repeat your name if you spoke up. You have to show callers that you control the situation. You're talking to them because you have a quality product to sell them."

A few heads turned. It was the same scenario as the previous day.

"Here we go again," said Abdoulaye, looking at Apollinaire.

Jacques stood up and laid his jacket on the chair next to Chrisosthome. He rolled up his sleeves and loosened the knot in his tie, like a man ready for a fist fight. Then he signalled Chrisosthome to take some calls.

He listened to the Burundian, walking in circles behind him. From time to time, he gestured rapidly to the trainee, reminding him to raise his voice, speak more dynamically, avoid pauses in the conversation. He wasn't to say "Yes, Sir" or "No, Ma'am," wasting time that could be spent on winning the customer. Politeness was for the weak. Jacques disconnected Chrisosthome's headset numerous times to tell him to sit up straight and stop being so polite. "It's not politeness that counts here, it's efficiency." Jacques's instructions seemed to go in one ear and out the other. Chrisosthome looked like a soot-black candle melting before everyone's eyes. His mechanical actions had a single goal—to make a pact with the devil. He tried to appease Jacques without really knowing how. Since he wasn't thinking, he made a lot of mistakes. When he did manage to sign up a customer, he looked up at Jacques to be congratulated. The supervisor merely gave him a half-hearted tap on the shoulder, like a trainer who doesn't believe in his boxing protégé and wants to get rid of him because he wouldn't make the first round.

VIII

How to End a Discussion

WHEN THEY FINISHED work, Apollinaire and Abdoulaye reported to Sébastien's office. The supervisors worked in the same long room as the attendants, but their workstations were set back. That way, they could watch employees unnoticed.

"Yes?" asked Sébastien, clearly interrupted by the two men.

"You asked us to come and see you before we left today," replied Apollinaire.

"That's true."

He pointed to a couple of chairs. Once the men were seated, the shark changed his expression to one of a father about to lecture two fidgety boys, both his own father's age.

"All the callers I spoke to told me that you were rude to them. I don't believe it," he was quick to add. "But I don't want to get that kind of feedback again. Otherwise I'll have to make out a report."

Abdoulaye shook his head, peeved. "Do you know what one of the callers said to me?"

"No. And I don't want to know. It doesn't matter."

"Yes it does."

Sébastien mimed that he didn't want to hear another word.

"He called me a dirty nigger."

The supervisor froze for a split second, raising his eyebrows. "I told you that I didn't want to know!" he repeated in an aggravated tone.

"But he insulted me!"

"So?"

Abdoulaye squirmed in his chair as if suppressing a strong urge to relieve himself. Apollinaire looked on without a word, ready to join his friend if he decided to punch the shark in the face.

"I had a lady tell me that I wasn't speaking English."

"I repeat, I don't want to hear any more about it. It's not my problem. If you're not happy, go and complain to the big boss. In the meantime, I want you to reread the model employee guide. There's a long section on ways of calming down irritated callers."

Apollinaire frowned. "Yes, but it doesn't say how to respond to someone who calls you . . ."

Sébastien sat up straight and leaned forward as if to hear more clearly what Apollinaire was going to say. The doctor didn't want to use the word *nigger*. That was blasphemy at this company. And in any public place for that matter. He'd seen people "resign" the day after uttering such a profanity in an argument with a customer. Abdoulaye came to his aid.

". . . rude."

"Is that what you were going to say?" Sébastien asked Apollinaire, with an impish smile.

"Yes."

"Here's a word of advice for both of you. Don't try my patience with your remarks."

"What remarks?" asked Abdoulaye.

The supervisor turned to the Senegalese. "End of discussion. You can go now."

The two men rose without another word and walked past curious co-workers who wondered if they would ever see them again. They rode the elevator in silence, each buried in his own thoughts. Abdoulaye stared down at the floor, his hands in the pockets of his large brown coat. The Sahelian's tall, lean physique had lost its gracefulness. Apollinaire clenched his fists behind his back. Shorter and more muscular, he looked like an innocent man handcuffed to prevent him from pouncing on his accusers. Their silence was laden, each thinking about what he would have done had he been able to defend himself. They were both thinking the same thing: that they would have leapt at Sébastien and pummelled him, calling him all sorts of insulting names. They thought about his smug manner. The most patient shark, he also proved to be the slyest. His face, although unpleasant, did not show any animosity, and his habit of admonishing employees far from inquisitive ears enabled him to avoid a reputation as fearsome. Yet his tolerant attitude somehow rang false and provided a trap for the naïve.

The doors slid open. They hurried through the lobby as if being chased. Instinctively, they stopped at the doors.

"See you tomorrow," said Abdoulaye, who exited and disappeared around the corner.

It was the middle of the night, and the traffic downtown had thinned. The whitish smoke rising from the tailpipes was adding to the hazy atmosphere. Apollinaire turned up his collar without thinking. As he was walking toward his car, he heard someone call his name. It was Chrisosthome.

"Would you like to have a coffee?"

Apollinaire shook his head. "My wife's waiting for me."

"Mine too."

The two men looked at each other for a couple of seconds, their faces tense with the cold, their lips bitterly stiff. Neither wanted his suffering to be discerned by the other. No admission of weakness, especially not between Africans. Their cultures, although different, shared the image of a man as stoic, self-composed and able to

41

brave any danger. How could they reveal the insecurity they felt without admitting that they were powerless in this society? The codes of conduct here were different. Their temptation to pour their hearts out was tormenting them, but their concept of a man would have never allowed them to confide in each other. This far away from the land of their ancestors, everything took on epic proportions. Confiding in each other meant accepting defeat at the hands of the civilization that built skyscrapers.

Without a word, Apollinaire climbed into the cab. Once seated, he heard Chrisosthome knock on his window. He opened the passenger door to let him in. Together in the taxi, they remained silent, the passing cars shaking the cab slightly. Apollinaire fought off a feeling of aversion. Toward the lame duck who couldn't accept that everything happened quickly in this country. The doctor couldn't bear the fact that Chrisosthome, despite his efforts, resisted the pressure that whites created in the workplace. He, himself, endured hurtful remarks from callers only too happy to remain anonymous. And he harboured anger toward supervisors, with their snide tones, condescending smiles and high-ranking officer attitudes. Yet he had learned to keep quiet, most of the time. He had built armour for himself that was as hard as the Canadian Shield. Why couldn't Chrisosthome do the same? Who was he to reject his fate?

The doctor finally turned his head and studied the Burundian's profile. His expression was that of a disoriented man. Apollinaire realized that his hostility was completely unjustified. It was only the foul weed that had grown in the hollow of his heart. He could almost taste the bitterness in his mouth. A kind of stench had developed within him.

"Back to square one?" asked Apollinaire..

"What do you mean?"

"You know,.in board games. The card you're always afraid of drawing."

"Oh that. Yes, but my life isn't a game," said Chrisosthome.

"Neither's mine," the doctor quickly replied.

Chrisosthome inhaled deeply. "I remember a movie called *Life is a Long Quiet River*," he said, glancing at Apollinaire.

The two men looked at each other out of the corner of their eyes. Grasping the absurdity of the title applied to their lives, they exploded into laughter. They howled on and on, clutching their stomachs, wiping their eyes, gasping for air. Outside, nothing had changed. Pedestrians were scurrying back to the warmth of their homes. For a brief moment, the two comrades had forgotten the cloudy breath of passersby, the dirty snow hardened on the sidewalk, the impassiveness of frozen faces. They had stepped outside of themselves, escaped their circumstances. Two gleeful witnesses to the absurdity of life somewhere in a parked car in North America. There was something universal about their laughter, and they had reached that no man's land where they could go beyond themselves. Suddenly, Chrisosthome's gales of laughter turned into groaning.

"My daughter's almost as old as Lynn."

"That's not Lynn's fault," replied Apollinaire softly. "She's just doing her job."

"And that damn Jacques. He's going to drive me crazy. I didn't sleep last night because of him. I curse him all the time. He's heartless."

"He's not paid to have a heart."

"But . . ."

"Look, they have bosses, too."

"Why are you defending them?"

"I'm not. I just understand their attitude. In their corporate culture, it's your neck or theirs. No getting off lightly. No compromises. You deliver, or they throw you out."

The doctor knew that the problem wasn't merely one of performance. His co-worker's angst stemmed from his view of the world and how people interact. But Apollinaire didn't want to address that issue. He felt too vulnerable and unable to confide in this man whom he didn't know well enough. He didn't want to tell Chrisosthome that, in this country, social norms don't involve hugging or extensive daily greetings. He didn't want to be the bearer of bad news—that leisure doesn't exist for the poor in these northern climes and that the promotion of a black is often a feat. Who was he to convey such a pessimistic message to a newcomer? Just an immigrant doctor. Apollinaire shook his head, as if struggling with some inner resistance. He opened the glovebox and took out a container of pills.

"What are those? Do you have a heart problem?"

"No."

"A kidney problem? Prostate?"

"No, nothing like that."

"It's Elavil. It's an antidepressant. I took a lot of it when I first got to this country. I still take it occasionally. I think you need it. Two pills a day."

The Burundian didn't look convinced. "All I want is to talk to someone."

"Like who?"

Chrisosthome remained silent. The question seemed difficult.

"Everyone's so busy, rushing around," said the doctor. "Of course there are professionals. Psychologists and all that."

"No, that's not what I want. I want to talk to someone who understands me. Not a white who'll check his watch so that he knows when to stop and give me the bill."

"What about your countrymen?" asked Apollinaire, suspecting the answer.

"They're too busy, too."

Chrisosthome began to sob, holding his face in his hands. The doctor gave him a tissue, then handed him the pills again.

"You really need these. Otherwise you won't make it through the winter. Keep alcohol to a minimum. It'll take you a few weeks to feel better. But sometimes the effect is faster."

"What do you mean 'feel better'?"

"You won't be as depressed."

The Burundian looked suspicious. "Where did you get these pills?"

"At the pharmacy. Here, I'll give you my number," offered Apollinaire, writing it down on a scrap of paper. "I have to go now."

Chrisosthome thanked him, more out of politeness than gratitude. The doctor was sure that he wouldn't take the pills, but his conscience was clear. He'd done what he could to lend a helping hand to someone in distress. After all, he, too, was in the lion's den. He started the engine and looked in his rear-view mirror. He would have liked to move on in life the way he could move out of this parking spot. It wasn't that easy. His life didn't have four wheels. He saw his existence more from the viewpoint of a swimmer exhausted from going around in circles under the impassive eye of imaginary onlookers.

IX

Last Stop that Night

APOLLINAIRE HAD LIED to Chrisosthome. He wasn't going directly home. He was calling in on a patient. The doctor couldn't abandon this man. He had to be at his bedside, if only for a few moments. It was a question of ethics. He still needed to believe that a doctor could comfort the dying.

The taxi headed east toward Regent Park. There was nothing seemly about this neighbourhood. Drug use, prostitution, robbery and gang violence were commonplace. People had to watch where they walked to avoid stepping on the needle end of a syringe. The buildings, bordered by dim walks and drives, were packed with the usual delinquents, who kept their hoods down over their eyes, more to avoid being recognized than to protect themselves from the cold. Apollinaire parked the car in a poorly lit section of the lot. He wasn't afraid of anything since the pimps and pushers in the area knew him. To them, he was the Doc. He wouldn't have been able to identify them in broad daylight in any event, because of the way they covered their heads. And the petty criminals watched him in secret, well back in the shadows.

"What's new, Doc?"

Apollinaire had barely put his foot down on the first step of the stairs. He recognized the voice. It was deep, almost a whisper. He could have never put a name to it, yet he knew he had spoken to the man before.

"Not much," he replied, without turning around. "I have something for you."

He slowly opened his bag, tilting it toward one of the only lights in the building that worked, and pulled out a box of condoms. A black hand grabbed it in silence. The doctor had to walk up to the third floor. Halfway up, another voice called out to him, this time a woman's.

"Hey Doc, it's been ages. Your dude's not doin' any better, you know. Don't go out no more. It's sad, man."

The doctor rummaged through his inside pocket and held out a pack of fresh syringes.

"Thanks, Doc. You're cool."

He turned his head to look at her.

"Don't look, old man. I'm not wearin' my Sunday best."

Apollinaire had time to glimpse her swollen eye. The girl wasn't even sixteen.

"Show me that eye."

"Buzz off, you old fart, unless you want trouble."

He heard footsteps receding in the hallway. She had already scurried off. When he finally reached the third-floor apartment, he banged on the door three times.

"Come in."

There was something hesitant in the voice. A weakness poorly hidden by a tone meant to be imposing. The one-bedroom flat stood in darkness. Apollinaire knew the place well and flicked on a light. The living room looked like a junk closet that had been hit by a cyclone, with crumpled clothing strewn about the cheap couch. Dirty dishes covered the small kitchen table, empty fast food containers filling every last space on the counter. An old

47

saucepan full of hardened rice sat on the stove, uncovered. Without further surveying the mess, the doctor walked through to the bedroom.

The only light in the room was cast by a small storm lantern at the foot of the bed. A man, his thinness discernible under the sheets, beckoned Apollinaire over. A strong odour of ether filled the room.

"Oh don't tell me that you're repulsed by ether, too. I use it to kill germs."

The doctor had the same worried look on his face as when he first entered the apartment. His friend had developed AIDS six months earlier, although he had been infected with the virus for much longer. Apollinaire had met him a few days after the onset of his illness, when he still managed to hide his symptoms. It was at one of those African gatherings that's organized for just about any reason. A stranger had walked up to him and said, "People tell me you're a doctor." Apollinaire had been surprised by the directness of the young man, who wasted no time admitting that he had AIDS and that he couldn't tell anyone else. He was taking his medications regularly, but would soon have to stop because they were too expensive. He had heard that Apollinaire might be able to help him. His name was Jean de Gonzague, but everyone called him WHO.

Jean was an orphan who had been adopted by a Canadian civil servant with the World Health Organization. The man had never managed to convince his wife that they should raise Jean with his two white brothers. So WHO spent his childhood in boarding schools, staying with the headmaster during holidays. His adoptive father visited him every week, and paid for all his education and living expenses. One day, his father was transferred to another country. From then on, their relationship was limited to letters, although his father continued to send him money. Apollinaire had heard about Jean back home. He was very popular, not only because of his athletic build, but also because he shared his Canadian money with his friends. Most of them were exploiters, but WHO had never known friendship for its own sake. His father, who retired in his native Alberta, eventually caught wind of Jean's carelessness with his money and cut off his support without further ado. He resumed his payments a few months later, after WHO convinced him to do so, then suspended them once again without justification. Wanting to clarify the situation and to see his father, with whom he'd had so little time, WHO boarded a plane, his Canadian passport in hand. He arrived too late. His father had passed away a few days earlier from cardiac arrest. In the meantime, his adoptive family had contested the will under the pretext that his father had written his last wishes after a number of heart attacks, when his cognitive skills were diminished. WHO had tried to see his adoptive mother and brothers, but they were never available. So he decided to settle in Toronto. He hadn't managed to communicate with the family in Alberta when his symptoms started to appear. The family lawyer sent him a few thousand dollars when he threatened to sue his adoptive brothers. Thanks to that money, he had been able to buy the medications he needed for a few months, but the funds had quickly run out because the drugs were so expensive. Apollinaire had become his supplier. He couldn't provide all the necessary drugs, but he knew that his friend was still alive because of him.

The doctor sat down on his bed. "You okay?"

"Yes, but your drugs aren't working anymore."

The doctor quickly opened his bag. "I think I have something else that will."

WHO swallowed with difficulty. He propped his head up slightly and touched his friend's forearm. "It's over. You know it, and I know it," he said, his tone serene.

Apollinaire pressed his lips into an awkward half-smile. "It's too dark in here," he announced.

"No it isn't. I wanted to do what we did back home. Use a good old storm lantern. You can even smell the kerosene. I lie here for hours watching the wick."

"Have you managed to get a little sleep?"

"Yes, a little."

WHO's gaunt face added to the gloomy look about him. His cheekbones stood out more sharply because of the dim lighting in the room.

"Who's been taking care of you?"

"You noticed the clean sheets, eh?"

WHO coughed noisily. "Shitty disease."

The doctor didn't reply. He took out his stethoscope, listened to his friend's breathing, and carried on the examination in silence.

"Tell the person who's taking care of you that you have to swallow these pills."

"No, no more pills. I've taken all kinds. I can't take any more."

"It's because of the pills that you're still here."

"That's just it. I don't want to be here anymore," he said without the slightest regret.

"Don't be silly."

"I've never told you my white name, have I?"

Apollinaire didn't understand.

"The name of the white man who adopted me when I was eight."

The doctor realized that Jean must also have his adoptive father's name.

"His name was Michael Strange. That makes me Jean de Gonzague Strange." WHO smiled weakly. "Isn't that ridiculous?"

The doctor didn't answer. Seeing the persistent look in WHO's eyes, he said, "It's just a name. Anyone could have ended up with it."

WHO shook his head. "No, I think it's a message from God. My life's strange. All the people who hung around with me when I had money are dead. Now that I have AIDS, it's like I live in a vacuum. I don't get it. The only ones who come to see me are pimps and prostitutes. They come here and ask, 'Where's the Doc?' I say I don't know, but I'm sure you'll show up soon. Then they smile and tell me their life stories."

"What, you think God's punishing you by inflicting this disease on you?" asked the doctor with some exasperation in his voice.

"No, I don't think God punishes anyone. I think he makes you realize that life is simple, that even petty criminals can show love. All the people who walk through my door care about me. It's too bad that I'm understanding life only now that I'm dying."

"Are your street friends the ones who are taking care of you?"

"Yes. Some of them are unbelievably loyal. They're sick themselves, but it doesn't show yet."

WHO shook his head, dejected. "Look at the way things have turned out. My father showed me that it's important to love and be loved, but he left my country too soon. I was only thirteen. I had to get along without him as my guide. Now, Ryan, one of his sons, calls me."

"Oh! So they're finally back in touch with you."

"Not exactly. Ryan calls me occasionally and asks me how I'm doing. He promises to come and see me every time. He lives here in Toronto, but he still hasn't come."

"He'll come," said Apollinaire, to reassure him.

"No, he won't. He's eaten up with guilt. Personally, I couldn't care less about his regrets."

"Are you angry with him?"

"No, I'm not angry. I don't let that keep me awake at night. I was born in the oppressed world, on the side that has nothing to blame itself for. I feel sorry for Ryan. He's lost. He doesn't know when to love, when not to love. He calls me and then he never comes. He's as hot and cold as his country. One day the government cancels a poor country's debt, and the next day it sends in paratroopers to impose peace."

"WHO, promise me you'll take the pills," pleaded Apollinaire, seeing nothing he could add to his friend's words.

"WHO can't promise anything, remember? WHO promised health for everyone by the year 2000. Well the new millennium is here, but children in the Third World are still dying by the thousands of diseases eradicated in the West."

He stopped to cough.

"Don't get worked up. It's not worth it."

"You're right." WHO laid his head back down flat. Apollinaire stood up and checked to make sure the window was shut tightly.

"You can tell your friends that I'll be back tomorrow. If you need anything, you have my number."

The doctor closed the door behind him. He knew he shouldn't discuss these matters with a despairing soul when he wasn't a specialist. To him, a hopeless man was like someone sinking in quicksand. You could get sucked down with the one you were trying to save. He did his best to convince himself that WHO wouldn't throw the pills away. He was secretly counting on his adoptive brother to come and comfort him. Yet Ryan's presence so late in WHO's life could have the opposite effect, and hasten his death.

X

A Doctor without a Cure

APOLLINAIRE DESCENDED THE stairs in the building, lost in thought. He felt powerless in the face of death—tiny, lilliputian before a gigantic monster, an unstoppable behemoth. He got into the taxi and, within minutes, was no longer a doctor. He had gone back in time and found himself in his mother's arms. A woman with very dark skin and deep lines. Why was he thinking about her at this precise moment? Because he was afraid of AIDS. He, a man of science, wanted nothing more than to take refuge in the arms of the woman who had brought him into the world. How could he be so helpless?

XI

Adèle, My Beloved

IT WAS MIDNIGHT when Apollinaire got home. Adèle was watching television in her dressing gown. He kissed her on the lips and removed his coat.

"How was your day?"

Adèle smiled faintly. "Nothing special. Same as usual."

"You'll never guess what the landlord showed me today."

She turned her head, waiting for him to tell her.

"An article he wrote about me in the neighbourhood newspaper."

"What did he say?" she asked, looking surprised.

"Oh, he talked about my situation. He wondered what the government's waiting for, why it doesn't do something so that doctors like me don't have to take odd jobs to get by. He also gave me this." Apollinaire unfolded the newspaper and took out the X-ray.

"What's that?"

He pointed to the name at the bottom of the film: Kevin Watson. "It's an X-ray of his leg."

Adèle shook her head, vexed. "That jerk wants a second opinion for free. It's not enough that he charges us a ridiculous amount for this dump. He has to take advantage of your expertise, too!"

Apollinaire felt his wife's mood changing and shifted to another topic.

"I saw WHO tonight."

"Oh, so that's why you're getting home so late. When are you going to stop playing the missionary?"

"I'm not playing the missionary."

"You don't have a licence. And where do you get those drugs?"

"Here and there," replied Apollinaire, looking down.

"I know you don't buy them. If anything happens to you," warned Adèle, pointing an accusing finger at him, "don't expect me to stand up for you."

He moved closer to her, wanting to make peace.

"We're not going to argue every day, are we? Let's not talk about it anymore. Okay?"

"That's easy for you to say," she replied, in a more conciliatory tone. She let her husband stroke her shoulders under her dressing gown.

"Do you remember the time we made love under your parents' dining table?"

"Of course."

They broke into laughter.

"Every time I heard a noise from the bedroom, I looked up and hit my head. I almost cracked my skull a number of times!"

Adèle chuckled.

"What is it?"

"I remember the time you told my father that he wouldn't have to spend another centime on his arthritis drugs if he'd let you come to see me."

Apollinaire shook his head, amused by the memory. "You can't imagine what I had to go through to keep that promise. I had to find a pharmacist who'd go along with it. I finally found one, but his conditions were steep. He wanted me to make sure that a hospital room would be available for any member of his family who ever got sick."

"Were you able to do that?"

"No. I had some pull, but not that much. Fortunately his family was in good health. And then he became friends with your father. At that point, I knew I had it made."

Adèle was no longer listening. She removed her dressing gown in front of him and went to lie down on the bed. Apollinaire followed her in silence. He moved his hands over her small, firm brown breasts and black nipples, then kissed her eagerly. He undressed quickly so he could continue fondling her. Adèle's incoherent murmuring excited him. He slid his fingers over her sex, covered with a silky black tuft, then wanted to caress her there with his tongue. As he brought his face between her thighs, he felt her hand on his forehead.

"What are you doing?" she whispered, her breathing erratic.

He understood that she did not want oral sex. Not wishing to interrupt the flow, he yielded to her, kissing her slender fingers. And when he entered her, she put her hands around his neck. He penetrated her as deeply as possible, the muscles of his firm buttocks contracting. As their rocking became more regular, Apollinaire could smell Adèle's scent emanating from her, like the essence of a peeled orange. With his eyes closed and his lips brushing his wife's feverish neck, he felt as if he had recovered his masculinity. It was the first time all day he felt sure of himself, of his actions. The watchful eyes of others had eroded his confidence, injured his pride. Self-worth always needs the appreciative gaze of a loved one.

These days, he no longer walked with confidence or charmed people with the sound of his voice; his accent made him self-conscious. He caught himself time and again bowing his head when a supervisor walked down his aisle. He was afraid. The passion of the doctor congratulated by his colleagues, the furtive admiration of the nurses assisting him, the smile of a patient who would have liked a husband like him, all belonged to the past. To another century. His self-esteem was now like a half-deflated balloon that regained its fullness only when he made love with his wife. He longed to do so, especially because, at the same time, he derived the satisfaction of being appreciated. He feared that one day his wife's desire would die out, like a volcano extinct for eternity. He would seem pitiful without a volcano to embrace his fire and no one to admire the nobility of his flame, to desire him unconditionally. This woman was his wife, and they loved each other deeply, yet he felt vulnerable, more fragile since coming to this cold country. He had been knocked off his pedestal, but making love to Adèle every night offered him a chance to win back his self-esteem. He felt filled with a mission—to have the fiery zeal of the ideal lover. He had to convince her that being relegated to the rank of cab driver didn't mean that he'd suffered the same setback in bed, the same spit in the face. Despite that, there was something sad about their lovemaking. A sort of the ritual, familiar but austere. He reached the shores of ecstasy, eyes closed, chest out, neck taut. Moments earlier, Adèle had clenched her fists until the last second, until she climaxed. Then they lay skin to skin, trying to prolong the amorous heat of their bodies which escaped gently, softly. He pulled up the covers as he came down from his pleasure, like a raindrop on a winding and unforeseeable path.

"The baby's like you," he said.

"How so?"

"She has the same bossy look when she wants her bottle."

Adèle grinned. "She made me laugh tonight. She saw a cow on TV and yelled 'Mel! Mel!'"

"She remembered the cow motif on her bottle. Tell me," he said, changing the subject, "do you really want to call her Nyngone and not Anne?"

Adèle smiled faintly. Apollinaire thought he detected a hint of annoyance.

"I want her to know her African name and to keep in touch with her roots. Isn't that what you want, too?"

"Yes, but Anne's my mother's name."

"I know, but Nyngone's my aunt's name."

The discussion ended there. Neither wanted to spoil this time together.

The telephone rang.

"I'll be right back," promised Apollinaire.

It was an overseas call.

"Apollinaire? It's Norbert. How are you?"

The doctor was surprised to hear his cousin's voice. He hadn't heard a word from him in two years.

"I was wondering how you're doing. How's the family?"

Norbert was the doctor's favourite cousin. He was the only one of his uncle's children with whom Apollinaire had developed a deep friendship when he moved to the capital. Norbert had escorted him around when he first arrived, and his help had been invaluable. The doctor felt indebted to him.

Norbert had dropped out of school very young and gone to work at a Lebanese store selling trinkets. Despite his meagre income, he had fathered a slew of children. Apollinaire didn't know exactly how many. Unmarried, Norbert visited the different mothers of his children at the end of each month to give them some money. The payments couldn't be considered support, because they didn't cover more than a week's food. They were more like proof of paternity, acknowledgement beyond a doubt. The mothers, proud to show the neighbours that, among their regular visitors, was a father worthy of the name, always managed

58

to attract people's attention when Norbert came by. They would call Norbert's child for half an hour, pretending not to know where he or she was. Or they would slip out for a few moments to run a supposedly urgent errand, so that Norbert could wait for them in the company of others.

Apollinaire heard Adèle growing restless in bed. He was bare naked, shivering with cold, but he couldn't break off the conversation. And he certainly didn't want to seem in a hurry. Norbert would have never understood. It must have been daytime in his tropical location. The doctor knew that mentioning how late it was in Toronto wouldn't have changed a thing. Norbert didn't pay any attention to that. Life in hot countries wasn't regulated by time. It was governed by strong emotions, births, deaths, prodigious fates and spectacular declines. Nothing else mattered.

"Apollinaire, your girl's sick. She's had a fever for the last two days."

The doctor knew that Norbert was referring to one of his nieces. He never used the word *niece*.

"Have you taken her to the hospital?"

"Yes. She has malaria. But there's no money for the Quinimax."

Apollinaire knew that malaria was merciless in Africa. Now he understood why Norbert was suddenly calling after two years of silence. He wanted help. He hadn't been in touch before simply because he hadn't felt the need. There was no ill intention on his part. Now that he required Apollinaire's assistance, he was asking for it. The doctor couldn't hold that against him. This wasn't the right time. In fact, he knew that there would never be a right time. He felt too guilty. Guilty for living far away. In the meantime, Adèle had gotten up to switch off the light and climbed back into bed, annoyed. The doctor didn't have any money to lend Norbert, but he would have given him the shirt off his back. He clasped the receiver between his open palms as if warming his hands by the

59

fire, and pressed it to his ear to bring his cousin's voice closer. Norbert's familiar accent lessened the distance between them, the time elapsed. Yet Apollinaire knew that this voice, infused with his adolescence, had the ability to burn him. He was aware of the power it had over him. A refusal on his part, even justified, could sever the umbilical connection between them. A mere hesitation, a somewhat awkward tone could break the bond they had developed over the years they spent together. His fondness for his relatives seemed, with the gap in time and space, like the edge of a cliff where it was perilous to tread. But his cousin still had the intonation of the lad who had protected him from the many dangers in their neighbourhood. Norbert was talking, but Apollinaire was no longer listening. He had only one question: how to hide from absence when it lands on your back like a raptor amidst the gloom. For his time far away from the fruit-splitting sun had indeed been gloomy. But he couldn't tell Norbert about his defeats. Norbert wouldn't have believed him. No one in a rich country, covered with a white carpet in December, suffers hardship. Not even snowmen.

"How much do you need for the drugs?"

Norbert replied plainly and precisely.

"I'll go to Western Union tomorrow and send it to you."

There was nothing much left for them to say. In reality, there was an entire world for them to recover. They would have needed to talk for a thousand and one nights to recall the precious times they had shared as boys, the moments of silence under the corrugated tin roof, the last snatches of happiness beneath the stars. There was none of that. Just a cold, abrupt click. With the years and the distance, their relationship had become grievously trivial. Their attempt at genuine conversation was more like a distress call in need of a response. Nothing of their fondness had come to light. All that remained were dying groans, which

Apollinaire tried to silence by depriving himself of the little money he possessed.

"So what was that about?"

"It was Norbert."

"I know. But what did he want?"

"A bit of money."

"I hope you told him we don't have any."

"I told him I'd give it to him."

The doctor knew she'd heard everything. She wanted to see if he would tell her the truth.

"You told him what? What about the rent?"

He didn't answer. Silently, he began to dress. Adèle climbed out of bed and clicked on the lamp in the living room.

"You just don't seem to be able to say no! How do you expect us to get by?"

"Watson'll have to wait," said Apollinaire in a hushed voice.

"Don't bring that old white man into this. This is about you. I almost think you'd be content to drive your friend's taxi for the rest of your life. Look at what we're living in! I married a doctor. Not a makeshift cab driver!"

Anne, who had been sleeping in the next room, started to cry.

"Now you've woken her up!" accused Apollinaire, pointing at their daughter's room.

"I don't give a damn!"

The doctor couldn't stay in the apartment. He would've started shouting. He had already decided to avoid any confrontation—he didn't feel capable of controlling himself. He managed to do that at work. But keeping a cool head at home was impossible. He had to leave right away. That's what he had decided, the day he realized that it would have done him good to hit Adèle. To beat this woman who kept telling him that she married a doctor and nothing else. To punch her, to shut her up. Just for a moment. To have some peace. And quiet. The walls seemed to be closing in on him when she yelled, "Where do you think you're going?"

She stepped in front of him when he tried to grab his pants off the chair. Anne, who was in her arms, began to wail.

"Get out of my way or else . . ."

"Or else what?" said Adèle, her eyes narrowing.

Adèle's creased forehead and stiff body angered Apollinaire even more. He resisted the urge to hit her. He had trouble understanding how he could go from making love with her to wanting to beat her, to bash her. He felt like battering her to the marrow of his bones. He clenched his fists, tensed his arm muscles and punched the air.

"Back off, for our daughter's sake," he ordered.

His raspy voice made Adèle step back. She looked at him, terrified. She had just understood that the man in front of her was not her husband. He was a stranger. Someone who looked like her husband. She slowly moved out of his way to let him get dressed. He felt her hand on his shoulder. He took it and squeezed it with all his strength. She winced with the pain. Anne howled, her head against her mother's shoulder.

"I don't know you anymore."

"I don't know you anymore either!" he bellowed. "Ever since we've been in this country, you've been harping on about how you married a doctor. Do I pester you? About being a cleaning lady at a hotel? No, I don't. Now get this into your head once and for all —I'm not a doctor anymore. I signed my death warrant as a doctor when I signed my immigration form. But I didn't know it at the time, otherwise I would've never left Africa!"

"And what did you expect to do back there? Play the martyr? Thank God Anne still has a father!"

Apollinaire shook his head, despondent.

"It's always the same old thing. You'll never admit that we should've stayed. Never! But that's what we should've done." He didn't believe what he was saying. He just wanted to silence her.

"How can you say that? You were the one who begged me to leave. You told me that you'd written political pamphlets signed "Schweitzer" and that the military wanted to kill you. Did you think it was normal for that black car to be following us everywhere?"

Apollinaire heard Adèle's voice reverberating in his mind, her intolerable litany. He stepped toward her and tried to take the baby from her.

"Give me the baby!" he ordered.

"No!"

Anne was sobbing herself hoarse, her small dark face covered with tears.

"She has nothing to do with this. Give her to me," he repeated.

"Let go of her!"

"Put her down," he ordered.

"Why?"

Adèle held the baby to her chest, protecting her as if a tornado threatened to rip her from her arms.

"Because . . ."

Apollinaire suddenly realized that he wanted to put Anne down on the floor so he could hit her mother.

"Because . . ." He couldn't bring himself to admit it. The words refused to come out. Unbearable pain gripped his throat and prevented him from continuing. He stood unmoving, his mouth half open. His rage had affected his ability to reason, and he banged on the wall out of anger and helplessness.

Apollinaire finished dressing and grabbed his medical bag. He was about to leave when Adèle's hand blocked the door. She was still holding the baby, whose wailing had subsided. She didn't realize that her husband no longer saw her; she was only a woman who had to be silenced.

"I'm opening a separate bank account tomorrow. If you want to give your money to Norbert, go ahead. But my daughter and I won't be out on the street."

"Let me out," he said, his voice distant.

He still felt the flood of anger raging deep within him. He had to leave quickly. He noticed that Adèle was trembling. He was shaking, too. He imagined her as so fragile, so easy to bring down. It would take so little to have her on her knees. An elbow to the ribs, another to the mouth he'd kissed feverously just a short while ago. Two punches would be enough. To shut her eyes. To end the stinking, spiteful, critical stares.

"I'm going to the Zanzibar," he hissed, yanking the door open.

"Yes, you're running off, as usual!"

Apollinaire went to leave, but a sound stopped him. Adèle continued berating him without noticing his astonished expression. He shrank back as two police officers, a man and a woman, started down the steps and were about to enter the small basement apartment.

"What do you want?" he asked.

Adèle turned and glimpsed the scene, stunned.

"We received a noise complaint from a neighbour. Can we come in?"

"Well you were going to anyway."

The policewoman headed over to Adèle, her gait stiff. Apollinaire stared at the policeman's cold face. The officer, remaining on his guard, did not take his eyes off the doctor.

"What's going on here?"

"Nothing," said Apollinaire. "Anyway, it's none of your business."

"When you prevent your neighbours from sleeping at night, it *is* our business."

The officer was tall, and his chiselled nape revealed freshly cut hair. He looked like a robot with his bulging bullet-proof vest. Adèle did not speak; she just rocked Anne, who had stopped crying.

"What's her name?" asked the policewoman, her tone almost affectionate.

"Anne."

"Nyngone."

The couple had answered at the same time. Their eyes met, and all the anger they were trying to hide behind the forced silence suddenly emerged.

"You and your white name. Her name's Nyngone! Tomorrow I'm going to change it officially."

"How dare you use that tone with me in front of strangers!"

"I'll use whatever tone I like with you!"

Apollinaire tried to go over to her. The policeman stopped him with a firm hand. "No. I'm the one you have to talk to here. What's your name?"

"Apollinaire Mavoungou. Doctor Apollinaire Mavoungou."

The officer acted as if he hadn't heard the correction. "Tell me how all this got started."

"I got a call from my brother, Norbert. She got mad because I promised to help him pay his daughter's hospital bill. That's all! You came here for nothing. I was going to leave when I saw you at the door."

"You were making enough noise to wake people up. If you don't stop it, I'll have to take you down to the station," threatened the policeman.

"Why?"

"So you can calm down there."

The doctor looked at the officer, trying to determine if he meant it. No doubt about it. He wasn't moving the slightest facial muscle, ready to respond to any resistance. Apollinaire looked down, resigned. The two officers in his tiny living room were attempting to resolve the hatred that filled him. The hatred of being humiliated every day to earn his daily bread. How could he explain the fierceness of his fury to them? Both officers, with their peremptory tone and thinly veiled disdain, humiliated him even more. The policeman told Apollinaire to sit down, which he did without comment. He had decided to cooperate and to avoid involving them in what they didn't understand—an immigrant's rage. The policewoman whispered something in her partner's ear, then turned to him. Apollinaire noticed their straight, intimidating posture. He tried to stand up; the policeman, his jaw clenched, motioned him abruptly to remain seated.

"Stay where you are. Do as we say, and we'll be able to leave in a few minutes."

The doctor furrowed his brow. He looked up at the policewoman, trying to understand what was going on. Her expression was difficult to read.

"So, your wife . . . She *is* your wife, isn't she?"

"Yes."

"She told us that you tried to assault her."

Apollinaire took the accusation like a punch in the jaw. He was ashamed and, at the same time, he couldn't deny it. He had to acknowledge it, to avoid completely losing face.

"Let's just say that I caught myself at the last moment."

The policeman smiled, incredulous. His partner looked at the doctor with contempt. Apollinaire could see in her eyes that, had the law allowed, she would have shot him like an animal. Her homicidal urge terrified him. He never thought that, one day, he would be petrified of people in uniform in his own home.

"We don't beat women in this country. It's against the law. You understand?" said the policeman.

"Doctor," added Apollinaire.

"What?"

"Do you understand, Doctor? I'm a physician."

The officer took a deep breath, showing Apollinaire he was striving to remain patient.

"I acknowledge," continued Apollinaire, "that I almost assaulted her. But I was going to leave when you showed up. You must take that into account. The fact that I've admitted it. Right? I mean, come on! *Merde!*"

Apollinaire let this last word slip out in French.

"*Maudit chien sale,*" hissed the policewoman.

"Speak English, please," urged the policeman, annoyed. "I'm having enough trouble trying to understand what's going on here as it is."

Apollinaire shot the Francophone policewoman a furious look.

"Do you know what she called me?" asked Apollinaire, outraged. "She called me a dirty bastard."

"I don't speak French, so I don't know. It's your word against hers." The officer went back to lecturing Apollinaire. "As I was saying, we don't beat women in this country."

"I know. I've lived here for years. This is my country, too. Just do what you have to do," said Apollinaire.

The officer tensed his jaw, a sadistic glint in his eye. "If your wife wants us to, we'll take you in."

The policewoman whispered Adèle's answer to him. "You're lucky, this time. She wants you to stay."

He gestured to his partner that it was time to leave. On her way out, she stopped in front of the doctor and said, "You lied through your teeth. Your wife said it was your cousin who called, not your brother."

"Well he's like a brother!"

The officers walked out, closing the door without a word. Then the door reopened.

"I hope we don't have to come back here. You got that?"

"Yes," replied Apollinaire, still furious.

He turned toward Adèle. He wanted to go over to her, console her, ask her to forgive him. He hadn't wanted to hurt her. It was so difficult for him to be the same person when he felt denied the use of his intellectual skills. He knew that wasn't what he should say to her. He didn't know what to do anymore. Nothing really made any sense. So he just stood there. He realized that he was still too angry with her to apologize. Why did she tell the officers that he'd tried to assault her? It was true, but there were things you should never say to strangers. To police officers. Especially white police officers.

"You know Norbert's like a brother to me. His daughter's very sick. I have to help him."

Adèle turned around, her eyes red.

"Your brother, eh? Well you can tell him to pay the rent to that old white man who called the cops!"

Apollinaire shook his head. "Why are you refusing to understand?"

"To understand what? That you're helping your cousin when you don't have enough food in the fridge yourself? I'm not refusing. I simply don't understand."

She headed toward Anne's room.

"Adèle?"

She turned around again.

"Why didn't you let them take me in?"

"It wasn't because of you, fool. It was because of that white policewoman. I'd rather she beat me to death than pity me. She thinks she's better than me. Their men are no angels. I see them at the hotel. They're as violent as anyone else. They just hide it better, that's all."

Apollinaire stood there, mouth agape. He finally understood that Adèle, too, felt the anger that gripped him, that she was infected with the same hatred. This gangrene was going to destroy their marriage, he thought. He had to act quickly. But he no longer had

68

the strength. He saw only one solution—to flee. He closed the door behind him. As he turned the key in the lock, he realized that, had both officers been men, he would have spent the night at the police station. Ironically, his wife, the irrational target of his anger, had just spared him further humiliation at the hands of the police.

XII

A Wife's Distress

ADÈLE PUT HER daughter down in her crib. She turned off all the lights, climbed into bed, and curled up in a ball. What was she doing in this country? It had to be cursed to have turned her husband into a violent stranger. Why did Apollinaire say he should have never left Africa? Hadn't he had enough of being harassed by the secret police? Or was he hiding something about his past? Writing political pamphlets and signing them Schweitzer was one thing, but having "unclean hands" as the rumour ran was quite another. She had never dared talk to him about his reputation. She thought such malicious gossip didn't deserve consideration. Now she wasn't sure.

She wanted to shout, "Cursed country, give me back my husband! But who could hear her apart from her own conscience, engulfed in darkness. "Take back this mad dog who's nothing like the man I married." The words stuck in her throat like ice in the neck of a bottle left out in the cold. She clutched the sheets, damp from her tears mingled with the musky fragrance of their amorous embrace. She sniffed the scent of her husband, the real one. Little did she know that, outside, the police were waiting for her Apollinaire.

XIII

Unfinished Police Business

APOLLINAIRE WAS STARTING the engine when he noticed the policewoman signalling him to lower the window.

"*Qu'est-ce qu'il y a encore?*" he asked.

"*C'est ton taxi?*"

"No, it's not my cab, but . . ."

"Let me see the papers."

"It's not my cab. It's a friend's. He's away on vacation. He lent it to me for a day or two."

"A cab driver on vacation . . . Give me the papers."

Apollinaire reached over and pulled the documents out of the glovebox. He realized that his medical bag was sitting on the seat beside him. The officers must have seen him get into the car. His heart started booming. His immediate reaction was to complain so that he wouldn't appear alarmed.

"Why don't you leave me alone?"

The policewoman, face tense, replied that she was only doing her job.

"You know very well that this isn't a stolen car. Otherwise you would've already arrested me. This is harassment. I'm going to make a formal complaint!"

The officer pulled her visor down to her brows and handed him back the documents.

"I've got my eye on you! Guys like you should be sent back to where they came from!"

Her partner reached the taxi at that moment.

"Relax! You can see that he's sorry. He won't do it again. Will you?"

Apollinaire shook his head.

"Get the hell out of here," she ordered, walking away.

"You'll have to excuse her," said her partner. "It's stress."

Apollinaire checked his rear-view and glimpsed her stepping into the police car. The policeman had inquisitive eyes. The doctor understood his ploy.

"I saw you leave," he said. "You seem to be in a hurry. Where are you going so late?"

"To a friend's. I'm going to sleep at his place, to cool off."

"Good idea."

The officer didn't look like he wanted to leave. A voice came in over his radio, asking him to respond to a certain code. He made an about-face and ducked into the police car. The vehicle disappeared, the siren wailing.

The doctor released a deep sigh. Despite the cold, he felt hot flushes rising to his face, a bead of sweat trickling down his spine, rigid with fear. Apollinaire sat motionless, trying to regain some sort of composure, a compromise between dread and serenity. He knew he had come close to disaster. Had the officers asked him to open his bag, he would have been discovered. Had he refused, it would have looked too suspicious. His night life, his only real life, would have been shattered. The consequences would have been dire.

Outside it was snowing. The sidewalks bore the footprints of people who had gone in every conceivable direction, toward their fate. Where was he going to tread? He smiled sadly. He felt lost, as if paddling against the current. Night provided a cover for his activities, but not for much longer. He was going to get caught red-handed or his wife would leave him, fed up with his lack of courage to face the day, to enter the shaft of light where she awaited him. Part of him had to die if he wanted to save his marriage and family. But did he still have the will to be a husband and father?

XIV

Did You Say Makeba?

T HE TAXI WAS still cold because of the time Apollinaire had spent with the window down talking to the officers. He tried to drive slowly despite his jangled nerves. It was difficult for him not to think about his brush with the police. He slipped a Miriam Makeba cassette into the player and began listening to *Kilimanjaro*, a bewitching hit. With the singer's magical voice, the music was as breathtaking as the snow-capped mountain in the heart of Africa. Makeba had the kind of pain vibrating in her vocal cords that draws listeners into the mist where their hidden sorrows lie. A survivor of apartheid, she sent forth her words like a priestess scattering mysterious beads. She projected her hazy breath, accompanied by very few instruments. Makeba had gone into exile, and was able to return to her country after the collapse of apartheid. Apollinaire didn't understand the words, but there was something subdued in the singer's emotion. Images of Makeba came back to him—her Nefertiti-like profile, her tall, lissome figure.

Decolonized Africa lived for so long in ignorance of South Africa that its impression of apartheid was similar to Western Europe's feeling about the Berlin Wall—horrifying but far away.

When Makeba burst onto the African music scene while in exile, she gave a face and a name to the millions of people corralled like animals in their own country. Makeba's voice contained unmuzzled life. In it, Apollinaire heard the tumult of oppression. He finally realized what was suffocating him. In Africa, he had always been on the right side of the fence. The only time he was in danger, he had boarded a plane. He had never understood this feeling of oppression until now, in his country of refuge. He was ashamed to discover Makeba's real pain so late and so far away. But there was no going back in time. Life wasn't a film you could rewind in a cutting room.

The song ended, and Apollinaire stopped at a diner downtown to buy a cup of coffee.

XV

Confidential Discussion

WHEN HE CONTINUED on his way to the Zanzibar, the city was a veritable blowing snowscape. Snow had collected in every possible place it could settle. It had been swept into immaculate downy drifts here and there on the streets downtown, hindering traffic. Vehicles were skidding; the few buses running were moving slowly. The courageous pedestrians out were unsteady on their feet. At a red light, a man knocked on Apollinaire's window and asked if he was free. The doctor hesitated for a few seconds, then decided to open the door for him.

"Thanks!" said the man, breathless. "I've been looking everywhere for a cab. You're the only one who's free."

He asked Apollinaire to drop him off near Roncesvalles, a Polish neighbourhood in the west end.

"What horrible weather," grumbled the man. "I've been in this country for thirty years and I still haven't gotten used to it."

The doctor responded with a polite smile. The man broke the silence again.

"What can I say? My wife's buried here. Most of my children work in Toronto. If I want to see my grandchildren grow up, I have to stay here. I don't have a choice."

The passenger's cheeks, red from the cold, were starting to return to their natural colour.

"Have you ever gone back to your country?"

Their eyes met for more than a second in the rear-view mirror. Apollinaire saw grey eyes dulled by time. He wondered what the man might have seen in his.

"Yes, but so many people were killed after I left that I didn't recognize anyone. It was as if other people had been asked to come and live in my homeland. They looked like my ancestors and spoke the same language, but their souls were different. No, everything's here for me. My memories—I carry them with me."

The doctor noticed deep resignation in the man's voice. Was he, too, going to wind up accepting this icy country because he didn't have a choice? When this country was no longer a necessity for immigrants, a refuge for the exiled, it became the depository of their emotions. Every cemetery in the snow preserved the memory of men and women who came from afar and never left. This country ended up keeping you through your emotions. It held you here through your heart and soul. It kept your children and your grandchildren. Apollinaire was thinking that he wanted to live and die close to his daughter. But how do you stay in a country that causes you to make a mess of your life? How do you explain to your grandson that his country of birth mistreated his grandfather? Wouldn't that be destroying what you'd worked for? Stifling the efforts of your descendant to integrate into this society? Showing contempt in a few scathing, spiteful words for the beliefs of a young citizen and, at the same time, crushing any redemption of the host country? The doctor imagined the man's long silences amidst the joyful laughter of frolicking children. Pangs of anguish, a lump in his throat, a hidden tear. Deep sighs between rides on a merry-go-round.

When they reached the destination, the man paid in silence and prepared to face the cold.

"I have a question for you," admitted Apollinaire.

The man seemed to have been caught off guard. He turned his head only to see that the driver had not turned his. He awaited the question, looking at the back of the driver's neck.

"Are you happy?"

The man sighed heavily, his eyes meeting the driver's in the rear-view.

"You know, I worked in insurance my whole life. I did quite well, and my children are settled. But I can't say that I'm happy. To me, being happy is waking up every morning and seeing the face of the woman I love, the woman I shared everything with. No country can get that back for me. Not even Canada."

He adjusted his scarf and set his hand on Apollinaire's shoulder.

"Even my children don't know what I just told you. And they'll never know. They think I'm happy. That's the main thing."

Apollinaire watched the man climb out of the car and take small steps toward a large snow-covered house. He went to turn off the top lamp, but realized he'd never switched it on. He was amazed. Was it providence that had put this man in his path? He drove away more puzzled than ever.

XVI

Manu Dibango Would Have Liked the Zanzibar

FINALLY HEADING TO the Zanzibar, Apollinaire changed musicians to change the thoughts swirling through his mind. He chose Manu Dibango, relaxed as usual. Lyrics barely audible in places, almost hummed. As if everything the Cameroonian uttered into the microphone had something unplanned about it. He could release a deep *ha ha ha* in the middle of a refrain, laughing freely, saxophone glimmering. There were also his monologues, unleashed as if inadvertently on a spicy note. He was renowned for his shaved head and the fact that Michael Jackson had taken a passage from one of his tracks. Africans needed no more than that to make him a legend. While the King of Soul Makossa did not like talking about the incident, his fans thrust out their chests with pride whenever Michael Jackson sang his version of Manu's *Makossa*. Apollinaire smiled, musing about it. There was something naïve about Third World pride, he thought.

True music lovers did not stop at that, though. They recognized his talent as a composer and admired the originality of his music, jazzy and thrilling. Manu Dibango would have liked the

Zanzibar had he been a Torontonian. It was a place where pockets of laughter would pop, like soap bubbles too heavy to rise.

XVII

The Zanzibar

THE MAIN CUSTOMERS at the bar were idle Africans who saved all week so they could treat themselves to a good time Friday night. The place wasn't much to look at. The smoke, hanging thickly in the air despite the ban on cigarettes, choked many patrons, who still clung to their drinks like a raft in the middle of the ocean. The pale blue neon ceiling lights added to the offbeat atmosphere of the bar, where people sometimes tripped over the sprawled leg of a slumped drunkard. The owner, the only woman not taken for a prostitute, ran the business with an iron hand. She had no fear of the boozers and braggarts. And she intimidated a number of them with her corpulence and piercing gaze. What sealed her immunity to any flak from the regulars was her past.

Colette came from the same country as Apollinaire. All the customers knew that she had been involved in "pavement radio" back home, earning her living by renting a calling card to anyone who wanted to make a call from a public phone. Long distance was expensive, so a card offered an affordable alternative. Not only that, the calls didn't appear on a statement, unlike those made from a cell phone. Colette used to spend her days downtown in front of telephone booths, calling card in hand. She knew everyone, from orderlies to ministers, who made incognito calls to their mistresses in shantytowns. The respect they showed her, tinged with mistrust, was due to the reputation of pavement radio people as informants. They were the eyes and ears of the most powerful. Zealous political officials would usually hear about any call criticizing the regime. How did they know everything that was going on? The pavement radio network supplied them with the most crucial information, from a plan to overthrow the government or the secret return of a former martyr, to an imminent student uprising.

Colette had left the scorching heat in her country, but her reputation had followed her. It stuck with her like the pallor of her skin, which had yellowed from the use of lightening creams. At the bar, no one dared argue with her about the tab since she knew every excuse for not paying. The customers deferred to her for fear she might remember some past misdeeds. After all, the regulars at the Zanzibar were no angels. Besides, it was better to maintain a good reputation in Toronto's African community. Anyone who lost that was doomed to stray outside the fold like a lost sheep. As a result, customers rarely fought and, when they did, it was never for long. The owner would simply raise her voice and they would fade into the shadows. Colette had heavy lidded eyes and black-lined brows. She wore a pencilled-on beauty mark by her mouth.

"There you are! I haven't seen you for eons. I thought you were avoiding me," she said jokingly.

Without waiting for a reply, she led him to his usual table. It was his favourite spot, dimly lit, away from the loudspeakers. That part of the bar was the epitome of ugliness. Greenish walls, questionable odours and drawings of scraggy palms. Yet none of that seemed to bother the customers, who were too busy with their drinks to take much notice. There was a man at his table.

"He's not in a very good mood," she whispered, as she walked away.

Colette was referring to Antoine Koumba, a former police captain seconded to the President of the Republic. His forehead shone under the sole harsh light, emphasizing the extent of his baldness. His narrow eyes, full of malice, did not move from his drink. But Apollinaire knew that the captain had seen him coming over. The man inspired fear in everyone: with his reputation as a torturer back in Africa, he made even the toughest people quake. He finally looked up when the doctor asked if he could sit down. It was merely a formality since the doctor kept him company every time they crossed paths at the bar. Apollinaire took a seat and shook the captain's extended hand. A hand that was narrow, slender, almost soft. Although his wrist was strong. The captain gave him a knowing smile, as he did every time Apollinaire sat across from him in that seedy place. The doctor responded with a barely audible "hello." Such a scene could have only occurred at the Zanzibar, he thought. A physician forced to conceal his treatment of patients and a former torturer compelled to go into hiding in the West. They were both afraid, but for different reasons.

The captain may have been living in exile, but no one at the bar believed he had changed. His cold, scornful gaze was just as sadistic as when he ruled supreme over the prison in the basement of the Presidential Palace. The customers at the bar remembered what they had heard about him. No one had seen him at work. At least, no one alive. He was said to have been surrounded by surly henchmen in a dank office, lit by a bulb hanging from a wire—a bulb that was constantly swinging. He was known as a tormenter who said little and never raised his voice. His silences were his cues to hit, burn or electrocute. His victims were not allowed to see his face. He kept his head in the shadows of the gruesome cells, behind the halo of the dismal swaying lights. His henchmen performed the dirty work with precision. They, themselves, were afraid that one day they might become his victims. When he was serving at the Presidential Palace, a few physicians had been hand-picked to treat the prisoners. Apollinaire was one of them. The two men facing each other at the Zanzibar knew that they had spent part of their lives in the darkness, in the shadows of a dank prison. The cries of pain, the thuds of bodies hitting the cold floor after rounds of electric shock, the howls of lunacy, the reek of urine . . . it all came back. Apollinaire bit his bottom lip, and the officer, looking pensive, turned his gold signet ring, revealing meticulously filed nails. No one had ever affirmed Koumba's acts of cruelty, but everyone at the bar was sure about the torture.

"Have you heard the news?" asked the captain with an enigmatic air. "The Minister of Finance is in prison. He diverted an oil tanker."

The captain signalled Colette to bring them the usual game.

"Are you talking about Okabi?"

"Yes, that's the one. Those new ministers don't know how to steal. They get too greedy, too quickly."

The officer looked disappointed, like a bettor feeling nostalgic about an endangered horse breed. Colette set the game of Scrabble on the table. Koumba loved the game. The doctor played for other reasons. At first, he had enjoyed beating the officer. The man was so feared in Africa that he would have never found anyone from his home country to challenge him, even in a game. Apollinaire was an exception. He still feared him at the Zanzibar, but he managed to control his fear. And every time he finished a match, he felt brave for all the times he had lacked courage. Not only that, Apollinaire's victories made Koumba less arrogant, less condescending. The doctor savoured the symbolic revenge. The officer hated losing. Yet it happened very often. So often, in fact, that one night when Apollinaire was about to beat him again, Koumba stopped playing and whispered, "What would it take for me to win?" Apollinaire was stunned. When he finally found his tongue, he asked the officer for a pen and piece of paper. He wrote down the names of all the drugs he needed to care for WHO, his friend with AIDS. And the pharmaceuticals to treat the wounds of the prostitutes from Regent Park beaten by their pimps, the ulcers of the customers who flocked to the Zanzibar, and the gout and syphilis of others. The captain glanced at the list without batting an eyelash and said, "Consider it done." From then on, every time Apollinaire needed supplies, he would slip him a list. The captain wouldn't even bother to read it. He would tuck it into his pocket and, at that point, he would win the game. The doctor had no idea where he obtained his supplies. Nor did he want to know. It spoke volumes about Koumba's shady connections, even this far from his homeland.

The customers at the bar watched the strange pair out of the corner of their eyes. They certainly suspected that the doctor had secret ties with the captain. But no one dared criticize Apollinaire because he had treated a number of them free of charge. Such charity, which they had never known in their country of origin, quelled any antagonism. And no one dared report Captain Koumba to the Canadian authorities. None of the patrons wanted to end their days in a dark alley in some North American city. They all wanted to live very long lives and return to Africa one day if circumstances permitted.

Playing Scrabble with the devil incarnate had its advantages. When Apollinaire headed toward a seat, the other customers would move aside; they never quarrelled with him or tried to sponge a beer or a box of condoms from him. The captain had penetrated the psyche of his countrymen long ago, representing terror in their minds. As vile as his reputation was, he also elicited their fascination because virtually everything about the man remained a mystery. Apollinaire would have never believed it had someone told him that, one day, he would be playing Scrabble with this death lord. When he saw the captain pull on his coat and

85

brush the snow off his windshield, he felt that he had been doubly duped. In his country of origin, he had learned to fear and obey the man. But beneath less favourable skies, Captain Koumba showed himself to be an insignificant individual with nothing more than a brush to clean the snow off his car. In coming to his country of refuge, Apollinaire had believed that he would be protected from torturers like Koumba. Yet here he was at the very bar the doctor frequented. Whether he had entered the country with forged documents or the collusion of senior Canadian officials was unimportant. What had disappointed Apollinaire was realizing that the land of plenty he had imagined didn't exist. The dream sellers who work for Immigration and Citizenship Canada had deliberately misled him. There wasn't a land of dreams anywhere. Now that he had opened his eyes, he felt deeply embarrassed for being so naïve. How could he have been so gullible? And to think that he sang *O Canada* loud and clear at the citizenship ceremony. How bitterly he regretted it. A country that denied an immigrant doctor the right to practise under the pretext that he had to take endless complex exams was no paradise. On the contrary, Apollinaire felt he was the victim of a form of torture even more vicious than that in his homeland. He would have preferred physical pain to the systematic refusal of an invisible tormenter to give him back his vocation as a man of science, as a human being with the knowledge to save lives. This intellectual suffocation was all the more brutal because he didn't know when it would cease. It wasn't like torture that stopped when the prisoner passed out. There was no end to Apollinaire's suffering. It was because of this realization that he could sit with Koumba and play Scrabble with him.

"Tell me, wasn't Minister Okabi one of your patients?" asked the officer without lifting his head. He knew perfectly well that the doctor had treated Okabi.

Apollinaire knit his brow as if trying to recall.

"Yes. I remember now that you mention it. Three sutures in the abdomen, multiple contusions, and fractured knees and ankles," said the doctor. "Your men really did a number on him," he mumbled.

"*Tsarina.*" The officer arranged his tiles to form the word, pleased with himself.

"Do you remember what his offence was?" asked the doctor, to irritate the captain. But he did not manage to do so.

"No."

XVIII

Koumba's Victims

APOLLINAIRE HAD NOT, in fact, forgotten anything. One morning, Professor Fabien Okabi refused to sing the national anthem. The man, so quiet, reserved and preoccupied with his mathematical equations, had cracked. He sat in front of his students, disgusted, waiting for them to finish singing.

One of them had reported him. Twenty-four hours later, his feet were secured to his ankles by a rusted iron wire, his head covered in blood. The punch wounds to the face had been sprayed with a cheap cologne called Magic Spring that the civil servants were crazy about. Apollinaire remembered the scent because he'd had to treat the professor's pus-filled wounds.

Okabi lost the use of his legs permanently. He had been delivered to Apollinaire like a parcel. Two men wearing hooded masks had dropped him off, bound hand and foot, at the infirmary. Okabi, groaning with pain, wore a note that read, "Take care of the perfumed prisoner."

A year after that dreadful incident, the professor was working for the government that had tortured him. In many tropical countries, redemption had the smell of money.

XIX

Scrabble and Irony

"I CAN USE the first *a* in *tsarina* to make *macabre*," announced Apollinaire, pleased with the irony.

The officer took a sip of his drink in silence. Colette appeared at their table.

"There's a call for you."

Apollinaire stood up and strode over to the telephone booth. It was Marcella, the young woman from his native village. Her husband had made off with the week's grocery money. He and his friend Wilson had resolved their differences and gone bar-hopping. Marcella was about to leave Nicéphore and take the two children with her. She couldn't tolerate his alcoholism and his abuse any longer. A week ago, after making some inquiries, she had obtained the address of a women's shelter. She gave it to Apollinaire, making him promise not to reveal it to her husband. He offered to pick them up with the taxi, but Marcella had already arranged for a ride and didn't want to wait in case her husband came home. The doctor promised to drop by the shelter to see her. He hung up, looking downcast. He felt ashamed for not having helped Marcella and, even more so, for having been violent with Adèle. Marcella's call made him realize how little difference there was between him and Nicéphore. He was walking down the same path. His relationship with his wife seemed to be slipping away like a fistful of sand.

In returning to his seat, Apollinaire learned from Colette that Nicéphore would be stopping by the bar.

"I don't want any trouble when he's here. If there is, I'll call the cops."

The doctor responded with a half-smile. Colette hadn't shaken the habit of listening to people's telephone conversations.

"Don't worry. You can count on me."

Back at his table, he immersed himself in the game again, paying no heed to Koumba's questioning eyes.

"I'm surprised that you didn't come to Minister Okabi's defence," remarked the officer.

"I'm a physician, not a politician."

"This country has changed you."

"Why do you say that?"

"The regime tried to make a dispassionate doctor of you. Now I see that Canada has succeeded where your homeland failed. You've become as cold as the winter here. I don't know how, in a country where people can spit on a head of state, you ended up becoming so indifferent to everything."

"I'm not indifferent. I've just never been interested in politics."

Koumba wasn't convinced.

"I have something to ask you," continued the officer, without lifting his head. "How did you manage to get the Stolen Choker back on his feet?

Apollinaire stiffened. He hadn't heard that name in a long time. "I'm surprised to hear that question coming from you, Captain. You're a curious man."

Koumba looked up, awaiting an answer.

"You were the one who typed the names Perfumed Prisoner and Stolen Choker. I saved more than half of your detainees."

The doctor pretended to be thinking about the captain's question.

"Oh yes, now I remember. His real name was Joseph N'Gouma. He was called the Stolen Choker because of the laceration on his neck, which was so deep you could touch his windpipe. Six hours on the operating table. In those days, the military hospitals were state-of-the-art. Not the civilian."

Apollinaire paused for a few moments.

"I can assure you that I wasn't the one who saved N'Gouma. It was his rock-solid constitution. The man took ten sutures, tons of antiseptics, and I was able to find a blood donor without a problem. You'll remember that he was an air force pilot. Those men are strong. I never knew what he was charged with."

"It's better that you don't know, Doctor Mavoungou."

"Can I at least ask what became of him?"

"Last I heard, he was living in Denmark."

"He must have a horrible scar on his neck."

Koumba smiled cynically. "Don't worry, he wears turtle necks."

With that comment, the doctor felt like quitting the game. But he couldn't. He needed Koumba.

The officer took another sip of his drink and set his glass down gently.

"Doctor, it's thanks to people like me that you were able to sleep at night. There was bedlam in neighbouring countries. You were able to practise medicine in our country without worrying about revolutionaries dropping bombs."

Apollinaire looked distracted.

"What are you thinking?" asked the captain.

It was Apollinaire's turn to make a word.

"I'm thinking that I should go easy on you. After all, you're the one who supplies me with meds."

"That's irrelevant, Doctor. You asked me for a favour because you realized we have things in common."

"I disagree."

"Oh come on, don't be ridiculous. To whites at three o'clock in the morning, we're exactly same. Here our past doesn't make any difference. Nor does our future," said Koumba. "You would've never dared to ask me for such a favour back home."

"That's true. I wouldn't have asked you for anything. But, here, I don't care how I look to people at three o'clock in the morning, white or not. I am what I am, and you're something else. And that's why I can face you here. Had I stayed in Africa, I wouldn't have stood a chance."

Apollinaire had felt the need to make this clear. Now it was an exchange. One favour for another.

"It's my turn to ask you something," said the doctor.

The officer frowned slightly. He wasn't accustomed to answering questions.

"How did you manage to get into this country? I mean, they do have a selection process."

Captain Koumba smiled, a spark of malice in his eye.

"No, Captain. I'm not asking you that to put you on the spot," said Apollinaire. "I wouldn't gain anything by it. On the contrary, it'd bring back too many bad memories."

"Don't be so sure. Memories often repress intentions."

The doctor didn't appreciate that comment. It stung him like a poisonous barb, infecting him with his own guilt. He had compromised himself before fleeing the country. He had dispensed care without denouncing the atrocities or always being able to save the victims. Why hadn't he fled sooner? He could no longer evaluate his remorse. Had it ever been worth anything? If so, what was it worth since he'd started playing Scrabble with Koumba?

"I got in under an assumed name, as you must have suspected. It was easy. You just need to know people with the African cooperative agencies to get a visa."

Apollinaire said nothing. That was all too enigmatic for him. He realized the extent to which this man could hurt him, even here in Canada. Koumba's vague answer had the strange air of secret dealings between rich and poor countries in the lobbies of four-star hotels in the West.

"Satisfied?"

"I wasn't expecting the revelation of the century."

At that precise moment, the doctor glimpsed Nicéphore and his friend Wilson making their way over to Colette. Their gait in no way revealed their inebriated state. The doctor asked the captain to excuse him—he wanted to talk to them. He went over to the two men, who did not seem surprised to see him. After the usual greetings, Apollinaire took Nicéphore by the shoulder as if wanting to speak to him privately.

"How's your cut?"

"Oh, it doesn't hurt as much now."

Apollinaire reviewed with Nicéphore how to care for the wound, then announced, "Captain Koumba wants to speak to you."

"Me?"

Nicéphore's expression changed immediately. He was not very happy about that.

"What does he want with me? I didn't even know he knew me."

The doctor didn't answer, but kept his hand on his shoulder. Nicéphore gestured for his friend to wait for him. Wilson continued talking to Colette.

At the table, the captain eyed Nicéphore coldly.

"Captain, this is Nicéphore," said Apollinaire, motioning him to take a seat. Nicéphore realized that the Captain hadn't asked to see him.

"Sit down," insisted Koumba.

"Captain, there's really been some mistake. I don't know why the doctor asked me to come over. I can see that I'm disturbing you. Apollinaire wasn't thinking, as usual."

"You can't insult him like that. Apollinaire's a friend. As you can see, we're playing Scrabble together."

Nicéphore swallowed hard. He suddenly started to feel very hot.

"Oh, I didn't mean to insult him. I was only kidding. The doctor knows me well enough . . . He even comes to my house."

"I don't remember hearing your last name."

"Ritangani. Nicéphore Ritangani."

"Ah! A man from the coast. I used to know a fellow with that last name."

"Boss, I . . ."

"Don't interrupt me when I'm speaking!"

Nicéphore shut his mouth and looked down as if fearing punishment.

"As I was saying, I used to know someone with the same last name. Poor man. He got mixed up in some money laundering scheme with a French company." The captain looked appalled. "Do you know what the people did to him?"

Nicéphore didn't move a muscle.

"Article 320. Three hundred francs for the litre of gas and twenty francs for the box of matches. Mob justice. So tasteless. I've always said that the masses are vulgar. Don't you agree?"

"Yes, Captain. Can I leave now?"

"Of course. This is a free country."

Before Nicéphore stood up, Apollinaire whispered in his ear, "The Captain despises people from the coast. If you lay a hand on Marcella again, I'm going to bring you back to see him."

Nicéphore turned slightly to look at Apollinaire, anger in his eyes. Then he scuttled off, quickly exiting the Zanzibar with

Wilson. Apollinaire remained on his feet, watching the two men leave. He could feel Koumba's glare on the back of his neck.

"The next time you need me to frighten one of your wimps, let me know beforehand. I'll be sure to wear my black suit. It has so much more impact."

The doctor slowly turned to reach for his coat, which he had hung on the back of his chair. He avoided meeting the captain's ironic gaze. Apollinaire laid the list of medications on the table.

"You can't get along without your drugs, can you?"

"Can you get along without being feared?"

Koumba did not reply, signalling the doctor to sit down. Apollinaire reluctantly complied.

"Let's stop annoying each another and speak frankly. I can get you reinstated in your profession for services rendered to the homeland."

"Here in Canada?"

The captain smiled awkwardly.

"No, not that. I know I supply you with drugs, but that would be asking too much. There are limits to what I can do, and this isn't our country. No, what I meant was, if you decide to go back, I'll make sure that nothing happens to you. And you can have your job back."

Apollinaire was tempted for a few seconds. But knowing that police officers of Koumba's ilk would show up at his door disgusted him.

"If I understand correctly, it's the same underhanded business back there."

"Careful, Doctor. It's not good to criticize the regime in front of one of its ardent supporters."

There was no threat in Koumba's voice, just impatience.

"Do you remember the Gutter Princess?" asked the doctor.

"Don't be absurd. There are things we should forget."

"Not that. Cause of death? Obstetric fistula. I remember her face. I remember her name. Julie M'Bama, fifteen and pregnant. Arrested at a demonstration by schoolchildren who hadn't had chalk or benches for over six months. Beaten and tortured. They made her abort in her cell. Her pelvis was too narrow, so they tore everything out. They brought her to me in shreds, Captain."

Koumba's face twitched slightly. He ran his hand over his bald head.

"I wasn't the one who had that file."

"It wasn't a file," corrected the doctor with impressive composure. "She was a young pregnant girl. I saw her die."

Koumba held Apollinaire by the arm as he went to stand up.

"Would you rather rot here, having to take one pathetic job after another? Yes, I know what you do to survive. It's disgraceful. These whites have got you all for a song. They welcome you with open arms, even give you their passport, but when it comes to letting you work in their consulting rooms, it's another story. Don't ever forget, Doctor Mavoungou, you're here to be useful to them, not the other way around."

The doctor finally rose from his chair. He was angry with himself for getting involved in such a reprehensible and destructive relationship. He was ashamed of needing a torturer. What hurt him most was hearing the same comments he'd made about this country from a criminal.

"It's time you got rid of your petty bourgeois pretensions, Doctor. Your remorse is that of an intellectual. These people ruined our country."

The officer finished his drink in one gulp.

"Human rights, freedom of expression . . . we leave that to the whites. There are lots of friends of Africa here! They pay attention to Africa's problems when they're on sabbatical and looking for a cause or when they see starving children on TV. If you gave me a month to take care of these fat little socialists, I'd ram their petitions, placards, white books and all their idiotic material down their throats."

Koumba realized that he'd just lost his patience with the doctor. That had never happened before. He didn't know how Apollinaire would react. And he had wanted to convince him to return home. His place couldn't be among a bunch of morons answering telephone calls from customers. The motherland could still get the doctor back, he thought. He shifted to a confidential tone.

"I answered the call of the State and so did you. Now another captain is doing the job I did, and another doctor is treating the wretches you treated. Life goes on."

Life goes on. The words reverberated in Apollinaire's mind. He left Koumba in a hurry, barely said goodbye to Colette, and walked out of the Zanzibar.

Outside, he fought the nausea welling up in him. Koumba galled him. The entire world seemed like one huge garbage dump. In the car, his mind turned to the captain's offer. His hesitation earlier embarrassed him. It showed how miserable he was in this country. He had to be distraught to contemplate a proposal from the devil himself. A helping hand, but one smelling of blood. How could such a brute sum up so well the ills gnawing away at him? He had no right to see so easily into his heart. Incensed, the doctor still considered turning around and telling Koumba he would accept. Leave. Flee this land that shone so brightly from afar, but became so dull up close. Escape this country of a thousand distorting mirrors. Everything seemed to take on dreadful proportions when you lived in these places. Winter crushed the roots of hope, year after year. The cold was colder, the snow thicker, people's faces more impassive than ever. In a labyrinth of ice, the sun, even offered by Satan, had salvatory rays. A hot hell versus a cold hell.

SILENCE FILLED THE CAR instead of the usual music. Apollinaire was driving carefully, letting hurried motorists moving at high speeds pass him on the slippery road. A few alcohol-dazed pedestrians looked like they wanted to hail him; the cold seemed to keep their hands in their pockets. The doctor wouldn't have stopped in any event. The top lamp on the cab was switched off. He imagined Norbert at the bedside of his seriously sick little girl. His cousin must have scraped together every possible centime before calling him. He felt obliged to come to his aid, even if Adèle was opposed to it. His brother was in distress, but there was more to it than that. He saw his financial assistance as proof of the ties that linked him to Norbert. Proof that he still belonged to a family. It was important for him to feel like a full member of a group, no matter how far away it was. How long had he been drifting like an abandoned boat? He had weighed anchor and followed an uncertain route with the sincerest intention of dropping anchor when he reached a place where he could feel at home. Yet he realized that he had packed up and left, without ever setting foot on shore. Somewhere along the way, he had suffered a shipwreck. But where? The landed immigrant looked more like a stranded immigrant. He had seen all his aspirations ruined because of bureaucratic indifference and the categoric refusal of a system that knew nothing about him, his dreams, his dedication. Seven years of training now counted for nothing, or very little. The sleepless nights spent studying on an empty stomach. Nothing seemed to matter: not his top-of-class grades, not his excellence awards. Despite all this, he still had to make his way through a mine field. Exam after exam, more assessments and submissions. He had never seen the light at the end of the tunnel. What do you do in a mine field when you know that you'll never reach the other side, that the nightmare will never end? You run around like a chicken with its head cut off. Apollinaire saw the years come and go, one after the other. In his mad, desperate race, no one could stop him. Not even Adèle.

WHEN THE DOCTOR arrived home, Adèle was sleeping in their bed. He took a shower and decided to sleep on the couch. The blanket there held his wife's scent. He stroked it for a long time, feeling confident. For a moment, he believed that he could work everything out. He dreamt that he saved Norbert's little girl and paid the rent on time.

XX

Late with the Rent

THE NEXT MORNING, Adèle didn't say a word. She ate her breakfast in silence, and he felt almost invisible. He didn't try to talk to her, because he didn't want to annoy her. Especially since he hadn't changed his mind about sending Norbert the money. Throughout the meal, he hoped she wouldn't ask him about it. He would have been forced to tell her that he was going through with the transfer. Apollinaire had a busy day ahead. He barely saw Anne, who seemed to have forgotten all the commotion the night before. He had to drop by Western Union to wire the funds to Africa and return the taxi to his friend Philibert N'Zumba, who was back from his honeymoon in the States. He called the babysitter and asked her to come early. Fatima arrived just before Adèle left for work. Apollinaire kissed Anne and, as he was walking out the door, asked Fatima if her foot still hurt.

"No, Doctor. It feels fine. I rubbed the ointment you gave me into my foot and changed my shoes. I'm not limping anymore."

He smiled without replying and closed the door, looking satisfied. Before getting into the car, he went up to the landlord's to tell him that he would be two weeks late with the rent. He rang once, and Watson answered the door, newspaper in hand. The house was in semi-darkness as usual, except the kitchen.

"Sorry to come by so early, but I thought I'd better see you before I run my errands."

Watson smiled politely. "You don't have to apologize. At my age, you get up early to make sure you don't stay in bed for eternity."

His humour seemed to amuse Apollinaire.

Watson's expression became serious again. "Come in."

He led Apollinaire into the kitchen where a copious breakfast awaited him.

"Did you want to talk to me about yesterday? I saw the police here late last night. I hope it wasn't anything serious."

The doctor refrained from saying that he knew Watson was the one who had called the police.

"No, it's not about yesterday. I hope we didn't disturb your sleep too much. Adèle and I got into an argument. You know, the way couples do. Someone called the police. But everything's back to normal now."

"Ah!"

Watson looked down, wanting to change the subject. "What is it that's so urgent, then?"

He motioned Apollinaire to sit down at the table across from him and his croissants. The doctor replied that he preferred to stand.

"I wanted to talk to you about the rent. Adèle and I are short this month. We won't be able to give it to you for another two weeks."

"Is that what you're looking so concerned about? There's no problem. I can wait," he said magnanimously.

"I can give you a postdated cheque."

"No, that won't be necessary. I don't think I'll starve to death in the next two weeks."

Watson stirred the cup of coffee in front of him, a reassuring smile on his lips.

"Beethoven? That's brave at this hour," remarked Apollinaire.

The landlord appreciated the doctor's comment. "You always amaze me."

Watson didn't know how much the music reminded Apollinaire of the basement in the Presidential Palace. The torturers often played Beethoven to drown out the groans of their victims. The doctor had never listened to the composer in the same way since.

"By the way, here's the X-ray you put in the local paper you gave me."

He held it up to the kitchen light, like a radiologist.

"Are you sure I can't offer you something?" asked Watson, pointing to his coffee.

"No thanks. I have a busy schedule today."

"What do you think?" he asked, after a time.

"Pardon?"

"Of my X-ray," said Watson matter-of-factly. "I put it in the newspaper so you could take a look at it. What do you think?" Still sitting, he took off his reading glasses which he had just put on.

"Mr. Watson, you know very well that I'm not a doctor anymore. Why would you ask me such a question? I can't give a medical opinion now."

Apollinaire wondered if the old man spied on him when he went out at night with his medical bag. He was afraid Watson might report him."

"Listen, it's my knee. I just wanted a second opinion, that's all."

Apollinaire didn't believe a word of it. "No, Mr. Watson. This isn't your X-ray. If it was, you'd be limping."

The landlord squirmed in his chair, trying to hide his embarrassment.

"I'll tell you why you gave it to me. To see if I'm really a doctor. After all, you defended me in your article. I seem to be some sort of cause you want to fight for."

"Come now, I'm not an enemy."

"That's true, you're not. But this kind of test doesn't make you an ally either."

The two men looked at each other in silence. Apollinaire went to leave, but he felt the need to tell Watson what he'd seen on the X-ray. He had examined it and had to talk about it.

"It's a case of osteopathy. In other words, a bone disease. If you brought the person to me, I think I'd be able to tell you more. Whether it's a tumour or a developmental abnormality. If I had to attempt a diagnosis, I'd say that it's osteopetrosis. It's hereditary. It often manifests after a fall. You see the opacity here on the X-ray? That's typical of this type of disease."

Watson scratched his chin. He felt exposed and ashamed. "I'm sorry."

"It's not the end of the world. But next time, don't use that kind of tactic. It doesn't suit you."

Watson didn't like that comment. "Surely you're not going to lecture me."

"No. But I will give you a word of advice. If you have any doubts about people, don't help them."

The landlord didn't seem to know what to think about that remark.

Apollinaire left the kitchen and found his way out. He had finally spoken his mind, and he realized that he hadn't been that frank in a long time. Why did he always show so much restraint? What prevented him from telling his supervisors at work that he didn't need their arrogance? Or the commiserating looks of some of them who wanted to be viewed as kinder? As if Apollinaire represented all the starving children they had seen in news reports on Africa. Kevin Watson, too, had a habit of assuming a distraught expression every time he learned that his tenant had to take another examination before he could practise in Canada. The doctor had never understood this incredible ability to show such empathy, without anything ever changing. The entire Western world must have moaned with grief every time a Watson defended an immigrant in his neighbourhood newspaper. Yet the moaning never got anyone anywhere. The Kevin Watsons of this country of refuge didn't have the ability to fight and ensure fairness for the orphan and widow. In fact, the Kevin Watsons of this host country doubted the competency of immigrants as much as the skeptics. Apollinaire had exposed his landlord's doubt and he was proud of it. This was an important day for him. He had been able to tell someone who claimed to be interested in his well-being that he wasn't fooled by it. But he'd had to catch him in a lie to do so. He wouldn't have another chance like this for a long time. Everything here seemed to be some sort of act, he thought. Was that really true? Or was he developing a form of paranoia that could eventually destroy his mind? All these thoughts were whirling through his head almost as quickly as he was driving to his friend's place, to the real taxi owner's. He decided to listen to some music to help him slow down, since the roads were still slippery. He chose a singer whose voice could melt all the snow around—Tshala Muana.

XXI

Tshala Muana, An African Reed

IN MANY AFRICAN countries, lighter skinned women could choose from a multitude of suitors who fell at their feet, awestruck by their fairer complexion. Tshala had that highly desirable colouring and a smoking-hot figure. Under the spotlights of national stadiums, she could create massive excitement among beguiled crowds. Not even the sound mixers, cameramen and other technicians supposedly at work escaped her seductive charm. Apollinaire remembered her skin damp with sweat from rolling her hips. Her voice was high and strong. The first notes the doctor heard in the cab reminded him of the time he climbed a tree to see her concert for free. He was not alone up there in the heights. Most of the shows in Africa had their share of non-paying spectators who applauded from their perch on a branch or their hold on a street lamp. The song she was singing had been a hit. It spoke of love, like most popular music, but with an undeniably African twist.

"I'm going to do a cowry throw. Touré will come back to me before Monday I know."

Africans loved these lyrics because they resonated with them, reflecting their world. For them, the small cowry shells were endowed with great magic power. They would go to see a fetish priest about life's sorrows and challenges which, of course, included love. Tshala Muana, elegant and electric. A reed that danced nimbly and gracefully. A blade twirling in the African wind. In the hot, dry and dusty harmattan of black souls.

XXII

Reunion and Revelations

PHILIBERT LIVED RIGHT downtown near the large shopping centres in a dilapidated building that seemed to have eluded developers. The grounds were well maintained though, as if to make the tenants forget that they were surrounded by government offices, banks and department stores. The newlywed lived on the ground floor. Apollinaire walked past an elderly woman who eyed him with suspicion, then entered the building without buzzing as some people were leaving. His friend came to the door the second time he knocked.

"Who is it?"

"Apollinaire."

"Schweitzer!"

The rest of his exclamations were drowned out by the clacking of three locks.

"Come in."

Philibert addressed the doctor in the national language of their homeland. The men were from different ethnic groups, but had both lived in the capital where they had learned that musical dialect. They hugged, exchanging the usual greetings and wishes, and asked one routine question after another about the family and their health. Philibert took his friend by the shoulder and showed him into his small living room. Bald and developing a paunch, he seemed contagiously good-natured. His very dark complexion and deep voice were becoming.

The living room walls were decorated with portrayals of peasant customs in varnished wood. The floor was covered with imitation leopard skin rugs here and there. Philibert had Western comforts as well—a sophisticated Japanese sound system in one corner that could play CDs and tapes as well as his LPs of old African music. The television had pride of place, with a larger than average screen. It was shiny clean like all the varnished wood furniture in the room. Philibert had even left the plastic cover on his couch so that guests couldn't soil the soft cushions.

"Where's your new wife?" asked Apollinaire in English. He didn't know if the young woman spoke their dialect.

"She's in the bedroom getting beautiful. She won't be long."

Then Philibert immediately asked the doctor in a light-hearted manner if he'd taken really good care of his cab.

"Of course. I mean it was very useful. Why do you ask? Is there a problem?"

"The police called me this morning to see if I'd lent it to you."

Apollinaire didn't reply for a moment. "That's odd. Oh, I know why," he said, it suddenly dawning on him. "It's because the police were at my place last night."

Seeing Philibert's worried look, Apollinaire gestured for him not to get worked up. "Adèle and I got into an argument," he explained in a low voice, so Philibert's wife wouldn't hear. "The landlord was the one who called the cops."

"Did you hit her?"

Apollinaire didn't like the question. But he knew he couldn't lie. Philibert had a sort of elder's right, and he was in his home. Still, he tried to be evasive.

"Not really."

"Tell me the truth, Brother."

"No, I didn't touch her. But I think things would've ended badly if the cops hadn't shown up."

Philibert clicked his tongue in surprise. "Why did you get into an argument?"

The doctor told him about his cousin Norbert needing money and what happened after his call.

"In any event, I'll be sending him the money as soon as I leave here."

"It's not right to hit your wife. But Adèle has to understand that you have to help your family when they're in need. As for the police, I don't think you have to worry about anything. I've been driving a cab for years. They won't do anything to you as long as you don't break the law."

Apollinaire knew that he and Adèle were going through a difficult time. He tried to dispel his fears about them separating by putting the whole matter out of his mind. His friend downplayed the situation, and the doctor appreciated his comforting words. Philibert, for his part, guessed that Apollinaire didn't need to be lectured or reminded of the truth. There was a tacit agreement between them—each could open up completely to the other, knowing he wouldn't be harshly judged. Advised to be more tolerant perhaps, but nothing more demoralizing than that. The doctor was very fond of Philibert. He could walk into his living room and, without going into any details, his friend could grasp the essence of his grief.

"Here are the keys. I've put gas in it.

"Wait a second. Why are you in such a rush to give them back to me? Let's just sit and talk first." Philibert opened his right palm and waited for his friend to slap it with his own. "Partner!"

He liked calling the doctor Partner. It was a custom in an Africa that virtually no longer existed.

"You look younger. Love's working wonders for you!"

Philibert smiled with satisfaction.

"Wait till you see her, Schweitzer. Flora!"

Silence.

"Flora!"

"I'm coming," said the voice of a poised young woman. The fifty-year-old seemed to relish the look of amazement in his friend's eyes when she appeared. Flora was taller than her husband and a striking beauty. Her face was like a finely sculpted mask, her features balanced, her chin narrow. She wore a green *pagne* over her slender figure, her gait attractively brisk as she went over to Apollinaire. She addressed him in English because she didn't know the dialect spoken in the capital. Apollinaire stood up and responded to her greetings, giving her a traditional hug. Flora was shy, but Apollinaire continued talking to her to put her at ease. When she didn't readily answer one of his questions, he moved on to another topic. There was about a thirty-year age difference between her and her husband. The doctor sat back down, trying to take his eyes off her.

"What would you like to drink?" asked Philibert.

After some hesitation, Apollinaire agreed to a glass of palm wine from back home.

"I have some good news. I'm going into business."

Apollinaire was surprised. "What kind of business?"

"Selling used clothing. It's very profitable."

"Do you have any experience?" asked Apollinaire, having difficulty hiding his skepticism.

"I don't need any. It's in my blood."

"You've been driving a cab for the past twenty years, and now you own it. You've just starting making a little money. Your experience is in driving a cab!"

"Schweitzer, stop being such a pain. I'm telling you that I know how to do business. It comes to me naturally! You know that my ethnic group has always been good at trade. It's innate. My ancestors dealt with the slave traders!"

"How much did the wedding cost you?"

Philibert suddenly looked anxious. "I'm up to my eyes in debt. I had to pay the dowry. Then I had to buy her wedding gown and the dresses for the six women in her family."

"What else?" Apollinaire wanted a full account.

"The plane tickets for the trip to Las Vegas, the restaurant tabs, the hotel rooms . . ."

"What about your in-laws?"

"They're poor and they've just landed in America."

"I thought it was only in Africa that you had to pay a dowry."

"Are you kidding? No, I knew about the dowry. It's the rest that got me into debt."

"I think you should give this idea of yours more thought."

"I've thought it through, Schweitzer. It'll take me ten years to pay off my credit cards. At my age," he added with a playful grin, "I don't think I have that much time to keep my young wife satisfied."

Apollinaire shook his head, disapproving of his friend's inopportune humour.

"You should have seen the look on her face when she saw where I live. She almost fell over backwards. She'd pictured something better than this. She's so beautiful, she deserves to drive around in a luxury car and dine out at chic restaurants like those people I met in Arizona."

"Who are you talking about? What people? Do they have a name?"

"Of course they do."

He whispered their name as if he was afraid lightning would strike him. Apollinaire knew the name. It was that of a rich family from his homeland. One of those untouchable clans that's weathered economic and political crises without losing its opulence. The clan was small but powerful.

"How did you meet them?"

"After the wedding, my in-laws suggested a restaurant. It was a very expensive place, as you can imagine. They were sitting near us. We ended up meeting them and talking. They're setting up stores all over the States. They asked me to be their representative in Toronto, and I accepted."

"Don't you think that was a bit quick?"

"No."

"You know those people as well as I do, Philibert. They might be rich, but that doesn't mean they any business sense. They lined their pockets back home by helping themselves to as much as they wanted."

Philibert signed to Apollinaire to stop talking. Flora came back into the room carrying a tray with two glasses of palm wine and two bowls of peanuts in the shell. Apollinaire admired her long hands and polished nails. She returned to the kitchen without a word.

"You see that? She's really fantastic," whispered Philibert. "When we talk about serious things, she makes herself scarce."

"Why don't you want her to hear what we're saying?"

Philibert cleared his throat, looking uncomfortable. "I told her that I owned a taxi, but I didn't tell her that I drove it or that I wanted to sell it. I think I was worried that her family might not agree to the marriage."

The doctor shook his head, disappointed.

"That wasn't honest."

"I know. Now I have to tell her that I'm the one who drives the cab."

He clicked his tongue, savouring the drink. "You like the palm wine?"

"It's delicious."

They sipped their wine in silence.

"No more housework. She's the one who takes care of all that now. She was raised properly, not like those women who want to be equal to men. You know, all those pains in the rear."

Apollinaire smiled without saying anything. He didn't feel like getting into a discussion. Every time Philibert started complaining about women, he ended up seriously disagreeing with him. Since living in this country, the doctor had discovered that he enjoyed cooking. He liked the idea of being able to fend for himself. When he changed his little girl's dirty diapers, seeing her smile made him forget about the smell. He knew that few of his compatriots would agree with his way of seeing things. To avoid alienating his friends, already so few in number, he preferred to live the way he saw fit and not talk about it.

"I'm going to sell my operating permit."

Philibert was talking about the document that enabled him to own his taxi—the document that took him ten years to obtain.

"You should wait for a while, until your business is up and running."

"Don't worry, Brother. I know what I'm doing. Look, I paid for the entire wedding on credit. I don't have any money."

"Why did you let yourself get into this situation?"

Philibert remained silent for a moment, looking down. "You know, I needed someone. As much as I need air to breathe. I don't know how else to explain it. Here, a taxi's just a taxi. But no man in this country will ever feel the way I do about Flora. She takes care of me the way she's been taught since childhood. She speaks my mother tongue fluently. She makes me good food from back home. What else could I ask for? It's perfect."

Apollinaire sank back into his chair. He saw the situation differently. To his mind, Philibert had worked like a madman for two decades so he could become a taxi owner. His baldness, sunken cheeks and rough hands bore witness to his unfailing endurance. He had washed dishes in restaurants, shined shoes and sold newspapers without ever becoming disheartened. Now that he was finally his own boss, he was choosing to compromise the fruits of his labour after only a few days in Arizona. What accounted for such a change? Apollinaire saw a worn-out man, with no one to whisper in his ear how brave and bold he had been. The doctor thought about all those long, monotonous, lonely evenings. He imagined all those days when he deprived himself of things to save as much as possible to buy the coveted taxi.

His love for Flora was like a need to offer himself a trophy while he still had time to enjoy it. He had fought a personal battle, and no one had given him a medal. The unknown soldier. So he was giving himself one. But not just any one—love for the aging warrior that he was. Before all his strength failed him, he had decided to take out love insurance instead of life insurance. Flora represented his revenge on this bloodsucking country. This country that had drained him of all his strength. Poor and indebted, he was nonetheless the husband of a beautiful, submissive young woman he should have married thirty years ago. Philibert finally felt like the ruler of his own domain. A man fulfilled by foiling the American dream. He had destroyed his sandcastle himself, indifferent to the criticism that might come his way. All that remained for him was to love his trophy. Love her with all his heart. Only how was he to do that? The truth was that he had to learn how to love again. All the efforts he had made to improve his situation had forced him to blind his heart. He hadn't allowed himself to love until he had saved the dowry for his soul mate. That restraint had made him a barren tree, unmoved by the gentle winds of happiness. But he was unaware of this wilderness within. All that mattered was his revenge for a life wasted, withered in the race to make money.

"I need cash, Schweitzer."

"You know I don't have any. I've even told my landlord that we'll be late with the rent this month."

"But you *can* do me a favour."

Apollinaire didn't like the tone of that remark.

"You're the only one who's friendly with Captain Koumba."

"No. Not that. Not you. You don't know what you're asking. And what can he do for you anyway?"

"He's loaded, and I need money fast. He can lend me some so I can pay off my credit cards."

"He's rich, but he's dangerous."

"I know, but I don't give a damn about his politics. It's his cash I'm interested in."

"No."

The doctor was grasping the extent of Philibert's desperation. He refused again, but not as firmly.

"Even if I find a buyer for my cab tomorrow, the bank will hold the funds from the sale for at least two months. I know how it works, and I don't have that kind of time. I'm up to my eyes in debt now. If I had to wait for two months, I'd be heading for divorce," he said in a hushed voice.

"What'll you give him as security? He won't want your cab."

"I don't know. And I don't care. I just need someone who has enough money to help me out fast."

The doctor studied Philibert's domed forehead and balding scalp shining under the light. They made him look older. This was the first time he had seen his friend in such desperate straits, and it upset him. He realized that he had become attached to Philibert. His friend had never criticized him for his activities; he knew the doctor secretly treated people, but that didn't seem to bother him. He preferred to talk about women and sex, or to tell anecdotes.

"Okay. I'll ask him."

"Thanks."

"Don't thank me. I don't know if anything'll come of it."

He already regretted his promise. He knew full well that it wouldn't get him anywhere. The captain was waiting for one thing, to return home. He wasn't a business man. His specialty had been interrogations that ended in murder. But Apollinaire didn't want his friend to lose heart. He had to help him remain hopeful.

He had never confided in Philibert that he had treated torture victims. Philibert called him Schweitzer like many of his country-men, but had never seemed curious about his past. So the doctor had never said anything. In any event, Apollinaire didn't think friendship involved reducing a person to being completely transparent. He believed it resulted from a unique mix of opaque sentiments that created a special dynamic. Philibert must have heard the rumours about Apollinaire, but they didn't seem to affect his feelings for his friend.

"Did you listen to the music in the car?"

Apollinaire smiled, amused. "You mean that old stuff of yours? Come on! You need some new tapes."

"No I don't. That old music is the best. You just don't want to admit that you liked it."

"You'd think that time had stopped for you. There are new African artists known around the world."

"What they're doing is garbage! I'm telling you, you have to have faith in the old ones. Look at Roger Milla."

"What about him?"

"He's an ageless soccer player. Give him a ball today, and you'll see what he can do with it!"

Apollinaire burst out laughing. "No way. Milla's all worn out. He's too old, especially in African terms. You never know exactly how old those athletes really are. Anyone can get a new birth certificate anytime at a central market."

"What are you taking about? said Philibert in all seriousness. "If someone gave me a ball today, even I could dribble it, no problem."

The doctor broke into laughter again. His conversation with his friend had taken his mind off his worries. He'd needed that.

"I have to leave. I have to run an errand before I go to work."

Philibert called Flora to bid the doctor goodbye. She thanked him for visiting. At the door, Apollinaire handed his friend the keys to the cab.

"No, keep the cab for now. I've rented a car for the week."

"I thought you were broke."

"I know. But I couldn't have her driving around in a taxi the first week after the wedding." Philibert sighed and adopted a confidential tone. "Listen, I know you need the car. Just make sure you don't get caught doing something illegal."

As Philibert was leaving the apartment, he called out to his wife. "Flora? I'll be right back. I'm going to see Apollinaire out."

They walked in silence to the building entrance. Philibert stopped and said, "I'll leave you here. I don't have my coat."

Apollinaire gave him a hug, then held him by the arm. "Are you sometimes afraid that you won't be up to it?"

Philibert held his gaze. He understood what his friend meant. "No, no problem that way. But I've gotten into some bad habits."

"What do you mean?"

"I can see that I'll have a few problems adjusting. You know a taxi driver has a "circuit." I can tell you the best places in town to get your *bangala* blown."

The doctor couldn't help smiling. He hadn't heard that word in a very long time. It made him feel as if he'd just received news from an old friend. Philibert certainly knew how to cheer him up. With just one seemingly ordinary word or deed.

"Do you mean your wife has never given you oral sex?"

117

"No," he replied hastily. "Her lips are just for kissing. The problem is, I really like it."

"Have you asked her why she doesn't want to?"

"She says it's disgusting. But I like it, Brother. I don't know who came up with it and I don't care. Maybe it was Satan himself. When something's good, it's good."

"Keep on trying, Philibert," urged the doctor, suppressing a smile. "She's young. She can change her mind."

"It took me twenty years to discover what a woman's tongue could do for me. I'd cringe every time someone offered. What an idiot I was. Needless to say, I had no idea what my tongue could do between a woman's legs either."

Apollinaire heaved with laughter.

Philibert continued with an even funnier straight face. "I don't want to waste any more time waiting for my wife to discover the virtues of oral sex."

Apollinaire wiped his eyes.

"Schweitzer, you're a doctor. What do you recommend?"

"Me? I'm in the same boat. I try almost every time we make love, but she's simply not interested. She thinks it's dirty, too."

"Really? Isn't there some little drug that can excite your partner?"

"Exciting your partner doesn't mean she'll agree to fellatio."

"Oh, you and your big words! What's *fellatio* anyway?"

"How is it that your young wife who's so submissive . . ."

"Submissive? She's not that submissive. She refuses to do what her mother told her not to."

"So you want a woman who's really traditional, but just not in bed. Come on!"

"I want to please my wife, and I want her to please me. That's okay, isn't it?"

"Yes, Philibert. Look, I don't intend to give up on my wife. I think you should keep trying with yours, too."

The two friends said goodbye again.

"A bit of advice. Don't sell your cab right away. Give it some more thought."

"A bit of advice for you, too. If you have any problems with the cops, don't panic. Just call me. I know a very good lawyer. He's so good he could prove that a brown squirrel bit a black squirrel because it was racist."

The two men roared with laughter.

"Believe me. I've seen him in action with a West Indian colleague. Picture in a Toronto daily, witnesses with tears in their eyes, the bad cops hiding their faces when leaving the courthouse. The works."

Philibert hugged his friend again and said more seriously, "This city's a jungle at night."

"I'll try to see what I can do with Koumba."

Apollinaire jumped into the cold car and glanced at the clock. He didn't have much time before going to work. He had to stop by the money transfer office as quickly as possible. Without a car, he realized that he would have had trouble running this important errand. Norbert had to be sleeping, since it was night in his part of the world. Apollinaire couldn't wait until he finished work to send the money; most of the transfer offices would be closed. He couldn't imagine driving all over the city at that hour to find one still open.

XXIII

That Morning at Western Union

BY THE TIME APOLLINAIRE arrived at the outlet, numerous customers had already converged. People watched him with irritation as he approached the line. One more customer. A teenage girl was standing in the queue, loudly chewing gum and listening to an MP3, her rock music audible even though she was wearing earphones. Apollinaire joined the line, looking resigned. He was afraid he would be late for work.

There was something uncomfortable about the wordless atmosphere in the office. Anxious, weary customers could be heard releasing sighs. Some were tapping their soles on the floor, reflecting a general impatience. The teller behind the wide, thick glass window was taking his time. The man he was serving did not look good: his winter clothes appeared to be cast-offs; his greying hair had not seen soap and water in a long time.

"One hundred and twenty-five dollars and thirty-four cents," said the teller.

The scruffy man took the money with an unsteady hand and counted it slowly, eliciting more sighs of impatience. He was shaking considerably, his red complexion likely due to chronic alcoholism. He finally put the money away and turned to leave.

He had not made it out the door when the teenage girl complained to the teller.

"We've got other things to do today. Why's there only one employee here in the middle of the morning?"

The teller lowered his glasses and interrupted the customer he was serving, signing to him to wait for a moment.

"Two other tellers ought to be here soon. Please be patient."

He did not show any irritation. His tone was professional and his voice, formal. He sat back down comfortably and continued listening to the customer, a man with Asian features. Apollinaire started to think that he shouldn't have dropped by Philibert's. In the line ahead of him were the teenager, two men in turbans, a woman wearing a veil and a white man with sunken cheeks and dirty nails. The longer time ticked by, the guiltier he felt about sending Norbert his rent money. He wondered if the others in this cold, impersonal place also felt a weight on their shoulders, as if their conscience had moved to a guilt-free part of their bodies as well. There was something ungrateful about Apollinaire's wondering if Norbert was really worth the sacrifice he was making. He shoved his hands into his pockets. These moments of hesitation made him uneasy.

Norbert had always treated him like a younger brother, and they had so much in common. But Apollinaire's inner voice challenged him to name what linked them so inextricably. He searched his memory for gems hidden in the rust that inevitably forms with time, but couldn't find any wonders he would have tucked away. He recalled a few unforgettable, touching moments, however nothing extraordinary. With the distance and the years gone by, they all seemed unreal, like a mirage in winter. Most of his recollections were buried in dust. All that remained was a desert of time and oases full of false certainties. The doctor was disappointed.

Apollinaire didn't notice the two other employees when they took their places behind the window. Both men sat down at their wickets, to the great relief of all those waiting. The line started to move more quickly, and the doctor was nearing the counter when he finally understood what he was doing. He was giving Norbert money to convince himself that he still had umbilical ties to Africa. He didn't have the means to help his cousin's little girl. The amount he was sending wasn't enough for the treatment to get her back on her feet. He was giving it to make himself feel better. He wanted to be at peace with a branch of the family he almost never heard from. Norbert had virtually vanished from his life long ago. And he had been the only one who replied to his letters for the first while. The others had slipped into oblivion, and the doctor into a sort of bereavement, without body or burial. He was annoyed with himself for not asking his cousin to explain his lengthy silence. He should have done so, but said nothing out of cowardice, the same cowardice that compelled him to answer Norbert's first distress call. Because he didn't want to take the risk of breaking family ties, even worn by time. Merciless time that undoes all ties, even those of blood, like a silk ribbon letting tresses fall into forgetfulness.

Apollinaire was rushing to his cousin's rescue in old worn clothes, those of an immigrant unable to meet his rent. Despite his poverty, he was racing to help this man who seemed more like a ghost than a cousin in Africa. To what extent should you let yourself be bled? Life isn't a bottle of sand you can open years later to recall the golden hue of the beach. It's an impassive current that can't be arbitrarily stopped without changing its course.

Someone tapped Apollinaire on the shoulder and told him it was his turn. He walked up to the counter, resignation on his face. He now had to pay the price for his illusions. He, alone, had finally understood the charade he and Norbert were playing. He had to go on with the pretense to avoid hurting his cousin. He went through the necessary motions at the wicket, convinced that he was not the only one in this situation. That's why a strange silence had settled over the office. People were nurturing ghosts to stop the rattling of the chains around their feet.

XXIV

The Greeting Card

THE CALL CENTRE was bustling. Some attendants were explaining the company's new offers to callers, others were filling out purchase orders, their eyes riveted on their screens. Latecomers were asking ill-tempered supervisors for instructions. Abdoulaye watched Apollinaire settle into his workstation, giving him an amused smile. The doctor wondered why his co-worker was looking at him that way, but said nothing. He thought it must be for a good reason, since Abdoulaye usually liked to greet him by cursing the impolite or impatient customers he'd had to serve.

"You owe me twenty dollars," he finally announced.

"Why?"

"Because of your friend."

"What friend?"

He nodded discreetly toward Chrisosthome. "He's leaving today."

He handed Apollinaire a card wishing Chrisosthome the best of luck. The Burundian hadn't lasted long.

"I guess I don't need to tell you to leave enough room for others to sign. You know the routine."

The doctor laid the card on his table, still shaken by the news.

"Bah! I never thought I'd hate greeting cards one day," said Abdoulaye, shaking his head. "But now I do. Talk about taking the bread out of people's mouths with a smile," he whispered. He quickly put his headset back on. A supervisor was eyeing him reproachfully.

Chrisosthome finally seemed to be working on his own. He was typing on his keyboard, but not taking any calls. No one was telling him what to do anymore. None of the sharks was paying any attention to him. Apollinaire, his headset connected but no caller on the line, watched the Burundian surreptitiously. Chrisosthome seemed relieved of an overly heavy burden. Their eyes eventually met. Chrisosthome gave the doctor a friendly wave, without fearing the stern gaze of the sharks pacing up and down the aisles. Apollinaire signed the card, without writing a message. He did, however, read what others had said. "It was a pleasure working with you" read one message in rough, tight script. "Stay in touch, don't be a stranger" said another in a feminine-looking hand. The doctor understood Abdoulaye's aversion to these cards: they were cruel when they came from an organization that fired you. He closed the card and passed it on to someone else, who would feel obliged to write a few words. Their employer insisted on it.

Abdoulaye told Apollinaire that he had asked Chrisosthome to join them for a drink after work. The doctor thought it was a good idea. A drink to his health.

XXV

A Tête-à-Tête

THE THREE MEN decided to go to a small café near the call centre. They chose a table away from the lights and settled comfortably in. The customers perched at the counter watched them take their seats. The waitress quickly went over to take their orders, since there were not many customers to serve. Chrisosthome asked for a beer, Abdoulaye a glass of wine and Apollinaire a whisky and soda.

"I thought that Muslims didn't drink," said Chrisosthome.

"My dear friend, let's just say that I'm not very observant," replied Abdoulaye.

They laughed heartily, the doctor looking on, entertained.

"You weren't with us for long. We didn't have time to get to know you very well," said Abdoulaye.

Chrisosthome became serious again. "That job wasn't for me. I tried, but I'm not able to pick things up as easily as I used to."

"What do you mean?" asked Abdoulaye.

"I studied engineering in Romania. Believe me, I learned the language in a year."

"Why Romania?"

"They were giving grants to students from my country," he explained, looking at Abdoulaye.

The waitress returned and set down their drinks, announcing the amount of the tab.

"I'll get it," offered the doctor.

"No, I will," said Abdoulaye. "It was my idea to ask Chrisos for a drink."

The waitress left with the paid tab.

"Jacques Dorion didn't let up on you, did he?" remarked Apollinaire, sipping his whisky and soda.

"He would've never treated me like that if we'd been in my country. To hear him talk, you'd think I'd never seen a phone in my life."

Abdoulaye and Apollinaire didn't make any comment. They preferred not to criticize Dorion. They were instinctively afraid of what they would say. They feared that they would reveal their disgust for him and the other sharks, with their devious monitoring, dominating stares and petty remarks. They had come to loathe these superiors in charge of counting the number of times they went to the restroom. Besides, Chrisosthome remained a stranger to them. They didn't know the real reason he was leaving. They had invited him for a drink, hoping he would tell them, his fellow Africans, why he was going. But the Burundian was tight-lipped. Apollinaire noticed Abdoulaye becoming somewhat impatient.

"How are things in Burundi? Is it still a dictatorship?"

"You know how hard it is for things to change in Africa."

"Well some countries are making progress. Is it in Burundi that the different ethnic groups hate each other? I've heard horrible reports on the radio."

"We're here to wish Chrisosthome farewell. Let him drink his beer in peace."

Abdoulaye smiled, looking embarrassed. "Sorry, Chrisos. You hear so many stupid things on the radio that you're happy when someone can give you the real facts," he said, trying to make amends.

The three men remained silent for a moment, each taking a sip of his drink to avoid looking the other in the eye.

"It's really late. I have to go," announced Chrisosthome, glancing at his watch.

"But you haven't finished your beer," protested Abdoulaye.

"I just remembered that I have a little errand to run before I go home."

Apollinaire stood up, smiling politely, and gave him a hug. "Good luck and all the best."

Abdoulaye embraced him as well, without a word.

"Thanks for everything," said Chrisosthome.

The Burundian pulled on his coat in silence, under the watchful eye of his former co-workers, and left the bar without looking back. Out on the street, his figure merged with the dozens of others lit by the neons of the neighbouring bars.

"That guy's a real asshole," said Abdoulaye.

Apollinaire didn't respond.

"It's not surprising that they settle things with machetes and machine guns where he's from."

"What do you have against him exactly?"

"He could have told us whether he quit or they booted him."

"Isn't it obvious that they booted him?"

"But why didn't he just come out and tell us? We're Africans, too. We have a right to know."

The doctor took a sip of his drink without replying. He was hoping that by keeping quiet, he could prevent his friend from becoming more riled. But Abdoulaye did not seem to be calming down.

"I've heard that the people in his country . . ."

"Stop it. You don't need to tell me about the people in his country. I'm not interested in hearing what you think of them. I can form my own opinion."

Abdoulaye took a gulp of his wine.

"I don't have anything against Chrisos. I just wanted him to tell me how he was fired, how it went. I want to know so I can be prepared in case those idiots decide to let me go."

"It went badly, like any firing."

"Yes, but I wanted the inside story. How did they tell him? In a letter? At a meeting in a boss's office? Which one? Was it that bastard Jacques Dorion, who told him with a smile? Or the beautiful Lynn Beatle, in her soft voice?"

"What difference does it make?"

"A big difference, Brother. I want to know who pulls the strings. They hire us, make us work, test us every six months, and we don't even know who the real boss is!"

"Yes we do. There's a message from one of the bosses every time the company makes a big quarterly profit."

"You know what I mean. There are bosses, and there are underlings who have a lot of power because the bosses listen to them."

"It wouldn't give you anything to know how it happened. Suppose it was Lynn who fired him. I don't see you telling her to warn you if they decide to boot you. Or were you planning on charming her?" asked Apollinaire with a teasing smile.

"No, but I wouldn't call her over when I have an angry customer. I'd choose my sharks better, to avoid being fired."

"Chrisosthome wanted to keep his dignity. He couldn't very well open up to two strangers."

"We're not strangers to him now. He's had a taste of what we do. He's felt what we feel almost every day. We're watched, we're listened to, and we can be laid off or fired just like that. So you know where he can shove his dignity!"

129

"Calm down. We're just talking, that's all."

"I know you agree with me, but you want me to do the talking."

Apollinaire finished his whisky without replying.

"I have two kids to feed, a wife who'd never put up with me being unemployed, and three other kids in Africa who think I'm rich because I live in Canada. I'm in my last year of night courses in computer science. So this is no time for some young blue-eyed woman to get rid of me because she doesn't like my accent or how slowly I speak."

Abdoulaye finished his wine and looked at his watch. "I have to run, Brother."

"Me too."

They stood up at the same time.

"Thanks for the drink," said the doctor, shaking his friend's hand.

"What about you? I didn't even ask you. Are you taking any courses?"

"Me? I haven't given up hope of being a doctor in this country. I've taken two exams, and I have to take two more. If I pass those, I'll have some courses to take. It's a bit complicated."

"You're either courageous or crazy."

The two men finally laughed.

XXVI

While Adèle Was Weeping

APOLLINAIRE SAT BEHIND the wheel but did not start the car. This was becoming a habit. He preferred to feel the cold cut through him like a self-inflicted wound. He was ashamed of still hoping to practise medicine in this country. He had passed his two examinations primarily because Adèle had worked two jobs so he could study. He didn't see how he could ask her to make that sacrifice again. Especially since it didn't mean that he could start to practise right away. He would still have to take some courses. He felt as if he hadn't been completely honest with Abdoulaye. Nonetheless, his hope was real. He clung to it, even though it seemed more and more like a pious wish. He put his hands on the steering wheel and winced. The cold stung his fingers and palms. He needed to feel pain. His shivering relieved the shame that gripped him. Yet somehow the cold did not seem as bitter as other nights. A hint of spring was in the air.

He and Abdoulaye should have never invited Chrisos for a drink. The Burundian had understood that they wanted to worm information out of him. Wasn't that even more absurd than writing meaningless messages on a greeting card? Apollinaire knew it was. He covered his face with his hands and shivered from head to toe.

He felt as if he'd been among hyenas fighting over some carcass. The hum of the traffic grew louder in his head until he couldn't bear the zooming. He opened the door, to stretch his legs and clear his head. A horn blared; he froze. A car skimmed past his vehicle in a gust of warm air. The doctor closed the door and started the engine. He needed to take his little girl in his arms. Anne was waiting for him, completely unaware of his distress. It was better that way, he thought.

XXVII

A Couple in Turmoil

POLLINAIRE SWITCHED OFF the music. So many thoughts were racing through his mind. He felt the need to make peace with Adèle and regretted not having done so that morning. She hadn't wanted to speak to him though. He still didn't understand how he could have reached the point he did. Did he need to start taking antidepressants again? The way he did when he first came to this country? He was annoyed with himself, especially for his lack of courage. He should have stayed with his wife after they fought. Why did he run off like that? He might have been able to convince her that he regretted his behaviour. He hadn't hit her, but it amounted to that. In Adèle's eyes, fate had stopped him in time. And to think that he had wanted to protect Marcella, a victim of spousal violence. He felt powerless over his own impulses.

Apollinaire was nearing his home when he had a premonition that Adèle wouldn't be there. He pressed on the accelerator. What would be left for him if she were gone? Pulling up at the house, he stopped abruptly, the tires screeching on the pavement. He barely took the time to park properly before jumping out and slamming the car door. Without locking the taxi, he hurried down the steps to the apartment. Looking for his keys took forever. Not finding them, he started to mutter. He noticed a glimmer under the door. That didn't mean anything. The apartment could be empty. He tried to calm down, and rummaged through all his pockets again. He hadn't found his keys when the door opened. He was surprised to see Colette's round face.

"What are you doing here?"

"Adèle called me and asked me to come over. Come in. She's waiting for you in the living room."

Adèle was wearing her night *pagne*, her hair braided in cornrows, revealing lines of her scalp. She had been crying and sat huddled on the couch. Apollinaire removed his coat without a word. The thought of Colette knowing about their marital problems irked him.

"What's she doing here?"

Adèle did not answer. She stood up instinctively, gathered her sleeping baby in her arms, and carried her into her room to put her to bed.

"You can go now, Colette. I don't need you here, to speak to my wife."

Colette shook her head in disapproval. "You shouldn't speak to me like that," she replied in his mother tongue. "I'm your elder and your friend. You could at least ask your wife why she's been crying."

Apollinaire was surprised. He had heard Colette say a few words in his native language at the bar, but he had no idea that she spoke it as well as he.

"I know why she's been crying. Because I used the rent money to help my brother back home."

He went into the kitchen to pour himself a glass of water. Adèle returned from the baby's room and sat back down on the couch. Colette took a seat beside her and held her hand.

"That's not why she's been crying," Colette called out. "She's been crying because you tried to hit her."

Apollinaire choked noisily on the water he was drinking. He didn't think his wife would talk to Colette about that. He considered her barely a friend, just an acquaintance really.

"Why did you go and tell *her*?" he shouted from the kitchen. The doctor's eyes were bulging with anger. He dropped his glass on the counter, and the women were amazed not to hear it break.

"Apollinaire, you don't need to yell. If you don't calm down, I'll be the one to call the police."

The doctor himself didn't understand why he was in such a state. Was it because he felt betrayed by Adèle? Or because he was ashamed that Colette knew everything, even that he'd tried to hit his wife? Maybe it was for both reasons. He pulled himself together for fear the police would return and take him away this time.

"I'm not here to humiliate you," began Colette in English so that Adèle could understand. "I think you owe your wife an explanation."

"What explanation? Even if I did, I certainly wouldn't give it in front of you."

His forehead was glistening with sweat. He clenched his jaw and rubbed his hands the way he did whenever he felt cornered.

"Who are you to tell me I need to explain anything?"

Colette gestured for him to lower his voice. "I'm a friend. I often don't charge you for the beer you drink at my bar. I'm your elder, and I've been beaten myself. Is that enough?"

Colette's voice was as cold as a blade at Apollinaire's throat. The doctor stood rooted to the spot, unable to escape her gaze full of suppressed rage. Colette sneered in disgust. Silence filled the room with a mute din as heavy as an anvil falling down a well. A fall that never seemed to end.

"Okay, I get it," conceded the doctor, breaking the silence to regain some control of the situation. Adèle, dumbfounded, watched her husband, his back to the wall.

"We fought because I promised to send my cousin Norbert some money. She kept nagging me about my decision. I don't know why, but I just couldn't take it anymore. She doesn't know how important Norbert was to me. He helped me when I first went to the city, and I owe him so much. I would've never survived in the capital without him. She kept pestering me and saying she was going to open a separate bank account. Then, I don't know exactly what happened. At one point, I wanted to hit her. I'm trying to explain this clearly, but it's not that easy. Everything's driving me crazy. Work, money problems. Everything's getting to me."

Apollinaire went over to his wife, who didn't move and cast venomous looks at him.

"I'm sorry, Adèle. I won't do it again. Ever."

Adèle felt a twinge upon hearing her husband's words. He had tears in his eyes.

"I'm going to open a bank account in my name. The money you sent Norbert was just as much mine as it was yours. I made beds and cleaned toilets to earn it. Thirty rooms a day, all on my own."

She stared at her husband and continued in a tone of contained anger. "I change tourists' sheets full of vomit, sweat and all the crap you can imagine. When I get home, I hurt all over. Life's enough of a struggle as it is. I don't need a husband who adds to it," she said, raising her voice, revealing the flood of emotion in her chest.

Colette took her in her arms and hugged her.

"This woman has made sacrifices for you," she said. "She's worked two jobs so that you could study and become a doctor for whites. She's washed the floors and cleaned the windows of the rich people in this city so that, one day, her husband could be what he'd always wanted to be. What do you do with all her sacrifices? You forget that she has an education, too. That she's a nurse. And have you thought about Anne?"

"Nyngone," corrected Adèle.

"Don't start that again," said Colette. "I'm older than you, too." Then she turned back to the doctor.

"Anne needs a father. But if you don't change your ways right now, she's going to leave you and take your daughter with her."

"No, I won't do it again," said the doctor, shaking his head. "I can't live without my wife and daughter."

He turned to Adèle and collapsed at her feet, covering his face to hide his tears. But Adèle turned to Colette and swore in her mother tongue.

"When I first starting working at the hotel, I felt so uncomfortable about taking tips that I deliberately left them behind when I finished cleaning a room. Now, I hate any jerk who doesn't leave me anything."

Apollinaire snuffled and bowed his head to wipe his tears.

"You two have no idea how lucky you are to have come to this country together," began Colette, looking at them in turn. "I had to leave my two children behind to emigrate. I was sent here to open a bank account for a minister, and I grabbed that opportunity to stay. My children are living with my sister. She's fine, but her husband's a drunk. I phone my kids regularly to let them know that the papers to bring them over will be ready soon. They're teenagers, but they cry like little kids every time I call. I don't know if that drunk is bullying them. They don't tell me anything. I guess they don't want to upset me, but I fear the worst. If he is being abusive, it'll be too late. The damage will have been done.

Adèle laid her hand on her husband's head, but he pulled back abruptly and straightened up. Seeing the tears in his eyes, she struggled to maintain her own composure. In a feverish tone, she managed to tell him something he had just sensed.

"I want you to stop treating people at night and to come straight home from work."

He lowered his head again, dejected, then turned to Colette, who was nodding in agreement with his wife.

"You're always out until all hours," continued Adèle. "We don't see each other anymore. We avoid each other."

"Stop! You don't know what you're asking me."

"I'm asking you to save our marriage."

"No. You're asking me to do the impossible."

Colette cleared her throat, to let them know she was going to speak. "She's right, Apollinaire. You can't go on like this."

He took a deep breath, striving to quell his tears. The harder he tried, the less he managed to control his emotions. His chest ached with unfathomable grief. He knew that one day his wife would ask him to give up what he was. He had thought about this moment so much that he had sensed it seconds before it came. He felt betrayed. Everything was crumbling. The last rampart against adversity in North America was finally collapsing. Adèle had tolerated his illegal practice because she hadn't wanted to hurt him. But she understood her mistake: because of his nocturnal outings, he had become a different man, a stranger. And that, she could not bear. She was telling him the truth now, just as she had when she objected to his sending Norbert money. For him, nothing in the world could make him give up treating people. A vocation acquired through a brave struggle could not end this way, in a dimly lit basement of a nondescript house. Tending to the ill and injured was his passion. If a government couldn't prevent him from practising, Adèle certainly couldn't stand in his way. It wasn't his fault that he received his training in another part of the world. In a place where people had the same organs as Canadians and their blood was just as red. He felt as if Adèle wanted to drain his lifeblood, hoping her love for him would stem the flow of his broken dreams. When you give up part of yourself out of love for someone else and nothing fills the void, you open the lid on a bottle of perfume and let the essence evaporate.

"I can't."

Adèle frowned. Apollinaire tried to avoid her inquisitive gaze, but to no avail.

"What do you mean?"

"Nothing. I don't mean anything."

Adèle sat up abruptly. "Apollinaire, I know you. When you won't look me in the eye, there's a reason."

"I'm a doctor. I'll always be a doctor."

Adèle turned to Colette, who understood that she needed to intervene again.

"People say things without thinking Adèle, and it doesn't matter. Your problem is making your husband understand that he has to give up his night life."

Adèle stood up, angry. She was getting ready to raise her voice. She looked at Colette, then at her husband.

"If you don't tell me what's going on here, I'm leaving right now and taking my baby with me. You'll never see me again. I don't know where I'll go, but I'll do it."

She glowered at Apollinaire.

The doctor ran his hand over the nape of his neck. So far, he had managed to avoid telling her about his past. Now, he didn't see how he could escape it. He had never imagined that he'd be forced to talk about that time in front of Colette. Yet she must have known about his former activities through her involvement in pavement radio. In fact, all the regulars at the bar had their suspicions, because of his habit of having a drink with Captain Koumba.

"I mean, I can't stop practising medicine. I can't do that for you. I've done other things for you, things I've never told you about because I wanted to turn the page."

"What are you talking about?"

Apollinaire glimpsed his wife out of the corner of his eye. He knew her well. This was the lull before a storm beyond compare.

"I treated prisoners in B4. For three years."

"You what?" she said, putting her hands on her hips, stupefied.

Everyone in their homeland knew what B4 meant. That place, somewhere in the Presidential Palace, had a reputation as terrifying as that of Captain Koumba. In the collective imaginary, B4 stood unsurpassed as a chamber of horrors. It conjured up images of blood-soaked walls and naked human beings hung by their hands or feet like refrigerated carcasses.

"Do you mean to tell me that you set foot in B4?"

Apollinaire shook his head. "No. They'd bring them to me in a nearby room at dawn."

Adèle cupped her hand over her mouth as if to stifle a cry from the depths of her being. Her husband avoided her gaze. She stared at him, stunned. Colette broke the silence.

"You two aren't acting like responsible adults. Adèle, I understand that you're shocked, but let him explain. And you, Apollinaire, sit down and start talking."

Colette made the doctor sit on a chair from the dining table. The couple were face to face but dared not lift their heads. Apollinaire preferred to look at Colette, who was seated by his wife.

"What do you want me to say? I treated torture victims. I washed, disinfected, patched up, stitched and dressed the wounds of people in shreds. If you want to accuse me of collaborating, go ahead. I don't give a damn."

Adèle started to cry. She wept noiselessly, just a small sniffle every couple of minutes. Colette held her against her imposing chest. "No, Adèle. Don't."

"Why are you crying?" asked her husband.

Apollinaire took his head in his hands and pressed his fingers to his temples as if trying to rid himself of a migraine.

"Are you crying because of what I just told you? I did it for you!"

He stood up, wanting to pace, but Colette told him to sit back down.

"Members of the Presidential Guard came to my office one day. They had photos of you. They never said they were going to hurt you, but from the way they talked about your beautiful face, your fine features, I understood."

The doctor looked up at the ceiling, recalling what happened.

"They had a photo of you waiting for the bus, wearing jeans and holding a handbag. You could see your slender figure and the shapely arch of your back. I said yes right away. And then I started to like treating those people. People you snatch from death. I liked that."

Adèle finally looked up at him.

"Why didn't you tell me? Why did you keep all this to yourself? Why?"

"The people who forced me to do that job weren't altar boys. I couldn't involve you. And I couldn't say no. If I'd refused or even hesitated, it would've meant two bullets in the brain for a loved one. That was their signature."

Adèle shook her head, trying to make sense of what she had just heard. It boggled her mind and overwhelmed her with grief. Who really was this man? Who was he? This strange person who had managed to conceal so many abhorrent things from her? Apollinaire took her suspicions like a stab in the chest. He clenched his teeth, furious.

"I didn't know the rumours were true," she admitted, distraught. "I didn't dare believe them."

"Adèle, he had no choice," said Colette. "You know how things work back home. You go along with them or it's over for you . . . and your loved ones."

"Whose side are you on?" asked Adèle, angry. "Don't you understand that he collaborated?"

"We all collaborated," replied Colette.

"No. Not me."

"Well, one of your loved ones, then."

Apollinaire understood, after listening to his wife, why he had fallen in love with her. He never tired of her integrity. She had a sort of aureole above her head. A diaphanous cloud of credulity. Even after arriving in Canada, she believed that her husband would succeed in obtaining his licence. Apollinaire, drawn under this halo of impalpable certainties, seemed to be warmed by it. He had been nourished by Adèle's light, like a plant oblivious to the drought seasons to come. She had always been a beacon in the tempest, the one who did not despair. But here she had put out her light, and the night he was navigating was like the darkness of the underground cells from his past, cells from which the groans of torture victims rose. Only the torture victim was none other than him now. Adèle had stopped hoping. The nightmare of her husband's past had caught up with her. The end of a dream in the dreamed-of country.

"I disgust you, don't I?"

Adèle didn't answer. Colette tried to reply in her place, but Apollinaire didn't give her time.

"I disgust you because I accepted injustice and murder. I witnessed suffering at close hand and didn't denounce it. I can see it in your eyes. You despise me."

The doctor rose slowly. All his anger was gone. Resignation guided his steps. He rested his gaze on his wife, who turned her head.

"The prisoners called me Doctor Schweitzer. Not because I wrote pamphlets. The truth is simpler. You want to know why?"

"Stop, Apollinaire," warned Colette.

Colette held Adèle, who had started to weep again.

"Apparently the old white doctor operated on Africans without anaesthetic in the colonial days. Too expensive for ebony. He'd just cut right in."

"Are you going to shut up?"

Apollinaire was not listening to Colette.

"The name stuck and followed me all the way here. Maybe it was one of those torture victims I saved. I don't know. It doesn't matter. I've seen one or two of the old prisoners from B4 on the street. They changed sidewalks. Shame maybe. I remind them of the torture they endured."

"Stop," shouted Colette, who was trying to dry Adèle's tears.

"Because even if someone saves you from a nightmare, you never want to relive it."

Colette told him in his mother tongue that it was time he left.

"Okay, I'm going."

He put on his coat without a sound. He didn't know where to take refuge. The Zanzibar was closed. Colette handed him her keys.

"You can sleep at my place. You know where it is, above the bar. Leave the keys in the apartment tomorrow. I have another set. I'm staying here with your wife tonight."

Apollinaire wanted to thank her, but the words wouldn't come out. He took the keys in silence and went to depart, but after a few steps, he turned around.

"It's strange. The people I saved often accused me, to avoid being sent back in for more torture. They said that I was one of them, that I'd plotted against the State. I saved them from death and they implicated me in their secret activities. At first, the authorities said nothing. Then, little by little, with one false confession after another, they began to have their doubts. They started tailing me and tapping my phone. I had to leave. I wondered for the longest time why the prisoners would involve me in their fate. Then one day I understood. They were afraid. They would have denounced their mother if they could have, to stop the torment. Fear won out. It destroys everything."

He paused and swallowed hard.

"If you're afraid of me now, Adèle, if you're afraid of my violence and my past, then I think it's all over."

He left without another word.

XXVIII

Night, Fear

APOLLINAIRE WAS ON his way to the Zanzibar, evanescent vapours rising from the storm drains. He didn't know if he should sleep at Colette's apartment or simply drive around. He no longer felt any sadness—talking had relieved him. Still, he suspected his sorrow was lurking somewhere in a part of his heart. For the moment, he felt soothed as if a balm had been applied to his wounds. His admission to Adèle had been anything but easy. Pain was always like a leap into the void. And he knew no way of preventing the impact to come.

The doctor stopped at a fast food restaurant to buy a take-out hamburger. He didn't get out of the car right away. He wanted to understand what had been plaguing him and grasp the root cause of his rage. Why had he tried to hit his wife? To beat her until he was breathless? He wasn't looking to blame anyone but himself. As a doctor, he knew that a radical change in behaviour is often triggered by a specific event. His flare-ups of violent feelings had started at work. He remembered that he had been asked to train a new employee, Lynn, the lovely blonde who became his supervisor. He showed her the ropes with the utmost patience. Barely more than a teen, she had been pleasant throughout her training.

But he knew from the moment he met her that she would be promoted over him very quickly. He and Abdoulaye had bet it would happen in less than a month. That whole charade had almost killed him, although he never showed it. He had trained others before Lynn, but she was the last straw, the one person too many. It gnawed away at him, and his anger turned to hatred. He fantasized about killing her by stabbing her in the head with a stake. Her blondness, red lips and affected pout almost destroyed his sanity. Fortunately there was Abdoulaye, who joked about the way Jacques Dorion smiled at her. Jacques inquired about Lynn's progress almost daily. Her errors were oversights, her laziness simply a hitch, her wretched French a splendid effort for a beginner. The doctor spent three weeks training her on the services the company offered. His calm, gentle voice concealed his tremendous urge to shout insults at her. He imagined impaling Jacques Dorion and frying Sébastien, the other supervisor, with electric shocks to the genitals. After all, he knew how it was done. He had seen the burns on naked prisoners lying unconscious in their own blood. His eyes had recorded methods that were unimaginable to anyone who wasn't a torturer. He acknowledged that he had wanted to inflict the same abuse on his superiors. His suppressed feelings of violence toward Lynn, Sébastien, Jacques Dorion and the others had surfaced against Adèle. Had the police not shown up, he would have made mincemeat of his wife. He knew it was true, even though it was difficult to admit.

When exactly had this cancer taken hold? Why had such hatred emerged from the murky waters of his life, like a leviathan from a dark lake? Why had the monster grown to such an extent that it wanted to attack the person he loved most in the world? He had been wrong to threaten Nicéphore at the Zanzibar. He thought it even ridiculous that he had tried to frighten *that* wife beater by sitting him down in front of Captain Koumba. Fear could only beget fear. He hadn't understood a thing. He had been repressing his own terror for so long. The echo of studded boots in the basement of the Presidential Palace, the rattling of prisoners' chains in lightless cells. Then the verbal abuse of callers, the intimidation of supervisors, the incompetence of subordinates promoted because of the colour of their skin and roundness of their buttocks. His fear had never died out. It had smouldered like embers waiting to burst into flames.

In leaving the restaurant, his dinner in hand, he stopped at a telephone booth. He was cold, but he still felt like calling Norbert. It wouldn't be too expensive since he had a special rate as an employee of a long-distance company. He put the meal in a bag at his feet and dialled his cousin's number.

XXIX

Norbert Has a Second Office

"HELLO," SAID A woman's voice. The line was clear. "Who is it?"

"Hello. Can I speak to Norbert?"

Silence.

"Norbert isn't here," said the woman in a friendlier tone, having realized that the call was long distance. "Can I take a message?"

"Yes. It's Apollinaire."

"*Ekié*! Apollinaire! Where on earth are you? Still in the land of the whites?"

The doctor racked his brain, but couldn't place her voice.

"It's Madeleine! Norbert's wife."

Apollinaire pretended to know who she was. "How are you?"

He was surprised that Norbert had finally married and that he hadn't said anything about it the other night when he called.

"You remember me, don't you? I used to live next door to your uncle."

The doctor remembered Mado, a little girl ten years younger than Norbert. The type of person who goes unnoticed and takes care of small children in the neighbourhood.

"Mado? Is that you? My goodness! So you married Norbert. I had no idea. He never told me."

"He's secretive, you know. He has a second office now. He's not the same anymore."

A *second office* meant a mistress. That wasn't surprising. Norbert had always had a number of women. He'd scarcely hidden it.

"Does he at least come home at night?"

"Not always! Sometimes his office keeps him all night. Honestly! I'm sure she's "drugged" him. He spends all his money on her and borrows more from his friends."

Apollinaire didn't believe his cousin had been bewitched. However, he now knew where his money had gone.

"Isn't Norbert's daughter sick?" he asked, no longer expecting that she was.

"No, Apollinaire. That's what he tells everyone so he can get money from them." Mado swore, using one of the coarsest words in the language of the capital. "I don't know what'll become of me. If he keeps this up, I'm going home to my parents. I don't even have milk for the children!"

"How many children do you have?"

"Four. Two with him."

"You have to talk to him, make him understand."

"That's impossible, Big Brother. I've tried everything. I've consulted the family, I threatened to kill myself, I even fought with the ugly witch. That cost me two days in jail! I finally went to see my *nganga*. He's the one who confirmed that Norbert was "bound" by another *nganga* allied with evil forces.

"Isn't there a remedy?"

Apollinaire was overcome by unhealthy curiosity. He wanted to know how far a distraught woman would go.

"Just one. He has to see my fetish priest. But he refuses. I can't seem to convince him that the woman's cast a spell on him."

The doctor's hands were cold, but he stayed on the line. In Apollinaire's ear, this dreadful situation resounded like a tropical refrain in the middle of winter. His considerable disappointment in learning that Norbert had wasted his money seemed to be eased by this story of bewitchment and fetish priest. In it, he recognized a frequent pattern of relationships in his native country. There was almost never simply a husband-wife-and-lover triangle. A fetish priest had to be involved. Upon him or her depended the final answer, the ultimate diagnosis of the cause of irreparable infidelity or deceit.

The doctor hung up. Feeling let down, he was angry only with himself. He could have decided not to send the money. He chose to do so even when he realized at the transfer office that it wouldn't do any good, that it wouldn't be helping Norbert, but only serving his own illusions.

XXX

From America With Love

APOLLINAIRE RETURNED TO the relative comfort of the cab and ate his hamburger, which had gotten cold. The engine was purring like a cat half asleep but ready to jump at the slightest sound. The tailpipe was emitting a stream of whitish smoke like a cigar burning out. He could still hear Mado talking about his cousin's dishonesty. He had fought with his wife for nothing. He should have never trusted his feelings. His mind turned to his family in the village, his uncle and cousins in the city, and the many other people who had mattered to him. His only memory of them was but a distant, immutable feeling. A set feeling remained true as long it went undisturbed. Norbert, in asking him a favour, had shaken this feeling and it had collapsed like a house of cards. Behind it, there was a lie. Apollinaire wiped his fingers on a serviette and stepped out of the car to throw the remains of his fast food into a garbage bin nearby.

Someone whistled at him as he was heading back to the cab: a man accompanied by a woman, shivering with cold. She was wearing only an evening dress, black stockings and high heels. The doctor noticed that the man was not wearing a coat either.

"I'm not on duty," he said, pointing to the top light which was switched off.

The couple continued walking toward him.

"Please. We're freezing. We left our coats in our car and we can't get in because the doors are frozen shut."

Apollinaire noticed the lady's jewellery and the man's white wing-collared shirt. A couple with money, thus a good tip. He refused again, although hesitating slightly.

"I can't take you anywhere. This isn't my taxi. It belongs to a friend."

He didn't know why he had admitted that to these strangers. Surprised, he decided not to say any more. The couple stopped in front of him for a few seconds. The man had brown hair, parted on the side. His sharp features gave him a hard, almost hostile look. He pressed his thin lips together, awkwardly trying to move Apollinaire to pity. His companion, who was short, took his hand and clung to him. Her darker, curly hair framed her small heart-shaped face. Her eyes, tearing with the cold, implored Apollinaire to do something.

"Get in."

The couple settled comfortably into the back, and the doctor asked where they were going. The man, preoccupied with the young woman whom he was trying to warm by rubbing her against him, quickly gave Apollinaire the address.

"It's in the east end, in the Beaches."

"Okay."

Apollinaire headed toward the Greek neighbourhood. He was still wondering why he had been so candid with these people. They must not have believed him. They must have thought he wanted to prevent them from getting in. Yet that was not so. He had preferred to be honest because he could no longer tolerate lying. The couple hadn't believed him, but that didn't matter. He drove along feeling lighter, without retreating into guilty silence.

In the back seat, the couple were kissing and whispering words to each other that Apollinaire couldn't make out. He glimpsed them in the rear-view mirror. They were clasping each other tighter and tighter. The doctor returned his gaze to the road, promising himself that he wouldn't steal any more glances in the mirror. But he was unable to stop himself. His eyes gravitated to the rear-view, quickly honing in on something intimate—his hand in her hair, a lustful embrace, parted lips.

"Stop that," he said, unable to keep his eyes on the road.

The couple paused.

"Are we bothering you?" murmured the woman.

"Yes. A lot. I could have an accident."

He shook his head, annoyed. He didn't understand why they couldn't restrain themselves for a few moments.

"We're not far from your place."

The woman left her lover's arms and leaned against the back of Apollinaire's seat. He could smell a flowery fragrance.

"Park over there and let the meter run."

The doctor pulled into an alley, which was deserted at that hour, and stopped the car. He didn't quite understand what was going on. Why keep the meter running when they were almost home? He didn't have time to ask, because the woman had already returned to her partner's embrace.

"What's going on?"

He realized, after asking it, that the question was absurd. It was obvious. The top of her black evening dress was unbuttoned, and the man's head was buried in her bodice. The couple started releasing low moans.

"Stop that! You can't do that in my car!"

"Oh, it's yours now, is it?" breathed the woman.

"No, but . . ."

"You can get out if you like. We won't be long," she managed to say.

"It's just that . . . Ah, shit!"

Apollinaire threw up his hands. He no longer knew what to say. It was cold out. He wanted to stay in the car, but he didn't want to hear or see anything. He put his hands over his ears and closed his eyes. He remained that way for about a minute, then he felt the couple's movements rock the car with disturbing regularity. The shock absorbers were shaking his pelvis, whether he liked it or not. He decided to open his eyes because he had been squeezing them too tightly, but avoided the rear-view. With his hands still over his ears, he quickly developed an erection. The continuous motion of the car and his back turned to the action were arousing him. He uncovered his ears and heard the couple whimpering on the verge of climax. Every sound made him want to watch more and more. His resistance was rapidly dissolving. He scratched the back of his neck, sniffled loudly and rubbed his chin, but nothing helped. His desire to see them was tormenting him. He had to look at the lovers. He turned around abruptly and saw the man with his tongue in his partner's privates. She was lying on the back seat, her pelvis raised, her legs circling his neck like a life buoy. The man was squeezing her buttocks, his mouth sliding up and down the contours between her lips, now iridescent. Apollinaire looked on with guilty pleasure. The woman was gripping the leather seat while jiggling her hips faster and faster. Her lover licked then stroked her clitoris with the dexterity of a goldsmith touching the smallest grail in the world. The doctor, captivated by the spectacle, felt a lone drop of perspiration run slowly down his forehead; he was warm in the midst of winter. The man lowered his partner's pelvis down to his own, penetrated her and withdrew almost immediately. He repeated the move, his back arched, withdrawing again. The woman, hungry for more, moaned, swearing at him. He smiled, delighted by his tactic. She didn't give him time to repeat it. She planted his sex within her groin, clutching his buttocks and wiggling her hips, up, down, left, right. Apollinaire witnessed the scene, stunned. The woman quickened the rhythm, the man plunging deep within her. She made love with her eyes closed and her mouth tensed. Then she told him to withdraw and move his head down. He complied, breathless. She rubbed his face eagerly between her thighs and, overcome with pleasure, went into an orgasmic trance. The man, who had been masturbating in the meantime, came on her evening dress seconds after her.

"Well?" asked the man, doing up his clothes.

"Well what?" replied Apollinaire.

"Did you like it?"

The doctor, no knowing what to answer, simply adjusted his rear-view.

"Tell us. We want to know," insisted the woman.

"Just give me the fare. I have to go."

He stopped the meter and extended his hand back to them without turning around. The man paid him generously.

Apollinaire was embarrassed. He felt like hiding until the couple had disappeared. He had liked it, but thought it improper to say so. How do you admit that you've been more carried away by watching two people make love than by your own relations? He had always believed that nothing could surpass the act of making love. Now he was no longer sure. It was as if he had watched the couple through the lens of a camera. His memory had recorded the roundness of her breasts, the curve of her hips, the pulsating of her buttocks, the outline of her slender back, the spicy scent of her pubis. These images came back to him like flashes from a video. He had made love with his eyes. It all made him uncomfortable.

"This was your first time, eh?" asked the man.

"Yes, it was his first time," replied the woman.

The doctor found his own attitude ludicrous. After all, he had thought that he was more open-minded than Adèle. Seeing was not having sex, he told himself. But he wasn't convinced. He felt strangely satisfied, like after making love.

"One last thing," he said to the couple. "Protect yourself against the deadly virus."

Apollinaire saw a smile on the man's still damp face.

"We're married," he replied.

They disappeared into the residential neighbourhood, hand in hand. The doctor was bewildered. Why would a married couple rather make love in a taxi than in their own bed? What did they find so exciting about being watched? What had happened to their sense of modesty? The greatest mystery, however, was the intense pleasure he had felt in watching them. He would have never thought that the sense of sight could thrill someone almost to the point of orgasm. Yet he was oddly certain that he had taken part in their lovemaking. All he had to do was close his eyes to see her feline movements, the shape of her legs, the dampness of her caresses, the cleft of her waxed privates. Apollinaire couldn't go to sleep after such an experience. He had to rid his mind of these feverish images.

He sat in the cab thinking for a few moments, the engine running. He hadn't simply been a witness to a lovemaking scene. He had, to some extent, participated in it. The lovers had been gratified because of him, because of his presence and his hungry gaze on their excited bodies. Without moving a muscle, he had fulfilled the couple's fantasy. He now understood the power of that word. He, in turn, had liked watching. Thus, it was his first experience beyond the strictly carnal act. This initiation shook his beliefs. He had always thought that the boundary of lovemaking did not extend beyond the limits of the lover's body. Outside those confines, there was nothing. However, this was not true: all the senses contributed to ecstasy. And to think there were millions like him on the black continent and elsewhere who were unaware of the potential of amorous fantasy. Why should the act of making love be considered concrete when the desire to love is abstract? The doctor did not have an answer. But he felt he had just learned that, despite all evidence to the contrary, the world was not round.

APOLLINAIRE DECIDED TO go and see WHO. The last time, his friend seemed to have lost all hope, and that had upset him. But he knew this patient. Some days were brighter than others.

The doctor wished he'd be in good spirits this visit. He realized that WHO was running out of time. He didn't have any more medications for him. Even if he did, they wouldn't have kept him alive for long. The virus, increasingly virulent, was devouring his immunity. Moreover, he couldn't tolerate the side effects anymore. Sometimes his upper back would swell or his face would bloat. Apollinaire had noticed that, although WHO was unable to keep track of the days, he still had his sense of irony.

The taxi arrived in Regent Park amid the shadows of prostitutes eyed by their pimps. The doctor parked the car and reached over for his medical bag. He had forgotten it. He had left the apartment in despair and his wife in tears. Questions welled up in his mind. What was he doing in such a dangerous neighbour-hood? More importantly, what was he so desperately trying to escape? He suppressed the urge to weep. Profound sadness weighed heavily on his chest. He drew a deep breath and stepped out of the car.

"Doc, got som'in for me?"

"Not this time. I forgot my bag."

The young man did not reply. He pulled his hood down lower over his eyes before retreating into the darkness of the parking lot.

"Got any syringes?"

The voice, verging on a whisper, paused in the dimly lit hallway leading to WHO's apartment.

"I don't have any. I forgot everything at home."

Apollinaire wanted to add something, but the person had already turned and left. He climbed the last steps to the apartment, worried. Without his bag, he felt so helpless, almost naked. He knocked three times because no one was answering. When someone finally came to the door, opening it only slightly, she did not invite him in.

"Sorry, Doc. WHO doesn't want you to see him in his condition."

"But I'm his doctor, and his friend!"

The young woman couldn't have been over twenty. An imposing man was standing back in the apartment. The doctor saw the tall, broad-shouldered figure creep toward him. He opened the door halfway, and Apollinaire noticed a scar running the length of his left cheek.

"Here, this is for you, Doc," he said, handing Apollinaire a white standard-size envelope.

"I want to see him."

"He's really not doing well. We're waiting for an ambulance. I know where you live. I'll keep you posted."

He closed the door without another word. The doctor didn't dare object. He stood motionless in the dusk, unable to make sense of what was happening to him. WHO didn't want to see him anymore. Why such rejection? His friend knew that he'd seen weaker bodies than his.

"Don't be so down, Doc," said a voice behind him.

He jumped in the semi-darkness. It was the young prostitute with the swollen eye he had bumped into the last visit.

"Everyone gets tossed out sometime."

He turned to face her and could smell her putrid breath.

"I can console you, Doc."

He tried to meet her gaze, but she lowered her head just before he managed to do so.

"No. I have to go."

He couldn't bring himself to leave. He sat down on the steps in the gloom.

"I hate men who cry anyway."

She disappeared without a sound, and he didn't know if she climbed or descended the stairs. He felt alone and abandoned by everyone. Adèle and WHO, not to mention Norbert, who had let him down. He remained sitting there in the darkness, dejected, his head bowed and his face in his hands. He reached for a tissue and touched WHO's letter. His desire to read it prompted him to leave this dreary place. He departed in silence, his hands in his pockets, protecting the precious envelope.

XXXI

The Encounter

EXITING THE BUILDING, Apollinaire bumped into a pale redheaded man rushing in, followed by two ambulance attendants with a stretcher.

"Are you here for WHO?" inquired the doctor.

"Pardon?" asked the redhead.

"Are you here for Jean de Gonzague?"

"Yes. What floor's he on?" asked one of the men in white.

"Third floor. Apartment on the left."

The attendants started ascending the stairs. Apollinaire held the redhead by the arm.

"Are you his adoptive brother?"

Surprised, the man motioned the attendants to continue climbing the stairs.

"Yes. I'm Ryan Strange. How did you know?"

The doctor introduced himself.

"He's told me about you. So you're the doctor," said Ryan, with some gratitude.

"Is this the first time you've come here?"

"Yes. But I've been calling my brother regularly."

"He's very sick."

"I know. I convinced him to go to the hospital."

Apollinaire asked him which hospital so he could visit his friend. As Ryan was answering, the doctor longed to know why he hadn't come to help his brother before.

"Why have you only come now? He's needed help for a long time."

Ryan, disheartened, ran his fingers through his thick hair.

"I don't know what he told you, but he refused our help. After the problem with the inheritance, when my mother contested my father's will, he didn't want anything to do with us. I don't blame him, but I didn't contest anything. I was willing to share my part with him. After all, I earn a good living. If you know him at all, you'll know he's stubborn."

The doctor nodded, a sad smile on his lips, and said, "It's too bad that money tears families apart."

He was thinking about Adèle being angry with him for sending Norbert money. A derisory sum. A deep wound.

"He told me that you're trying to get a licence to practise in Canada."

"Yes."

"It's hard. The regulations here are so strict."

He looked concerned about Apollinaire's fate. The doctor imagined that he was dealing with another Watson.

"I'd like to ask you something," said Apollinaire.

Ryan smiled politely.

"Did your father have to get his equivalence for his Canadian degree when he was working in Africa?"

"No. But he wasn't practising. He was a civil servant for an international organization."

"Yes, but he was giving seminars to physicians and courses on viral diseases. I know because I attended the one on the recrudescence of poliomyelitis."

Ryan nodded, admitting, "In any case, there were foreign doctors who were practising."

"Well?"

"Listen, I don't know why it's so complicated here. If I were you, I wouldn't take it lying down."

The doctor didn't have time to reply. The ambulance attendants walked past them wheeling WHO on the stretcher. Apollinaire glimpsed only his recumbent silhouette in the twilight. Ryan followed them, and the doctor stood there in front of the building, watching the wailing ambulance turn onto the dark, empty street.

XXXII

The Affliction Invented to Deter Sweethearts (AIDS)

POLLINAIRE PARKED THE cab in an alley near the downtown core. He had managed to find a lighted spot next to the Zanzibar and opened WHO's letter.

Schweitzer,

I've never felt so bad in my whole life. It's not easy to tell someone who tried to keep you alive that he was wasting his time. But I have to tell you, Schweitzer. You wasted your time running after drugs that were supposed to do me good. They didn't help; they gave me false hope and side effects. I should have told you not to come anymore because I've been throwing the pills in the garbage for the last few weeks. But you seemed to like what you were doing so much that it was difficult to turn you down. I don't want your help anymore though. I know you don't have any more drugs for me, but it's not the pills that kept me alive. It was your devotion. Your caring prevented the life in me from draining away, like beads of sweat through my pores. It still dwindled, but politely, as if apologizing for leaving me.

You're haunted by the people who were tortured at the Presidential Palace. Yes, I know about that, as do many of our countrymen. But this isn't the time for laying blame, if ever there was one. You have to stop coming to see me, to chase away your demons. No one can help you but yourself. Reality is cruel, especially when you turn your back on it. Since I'm facing my fate, you can face yours. You're no longer a doctor and, soon, I'll no longer be alive. I'm waiting for the darkness and you're waiting only for the dawn. Your compassion doesn't need a medical degree, Schweitzer. You're worth a lot more than their piece of paper. Happiness isn't found on a diploma.

Since I've hurt you, I have a duty to tell you my biggest secret. I have to let you know what I dream about here on my sickbed, what makes me happy in daytime and miserable at night. Sabrina had large, deep black eyes and a small nose that rounded when she smiled. She had the irresistible charm of the women from the coast—short and slender, with round buttocks and tiny feet. That old undeclared flame was rekindled, almost by accident. A bar, a seated woman and a back that I recognized and that beckoned me. The smile upon our reunion and the inability to part without a promise to meet again. Every morning, lying in bed, I see her kiss my lips, her *pagne* around her hips, her chest bare. It wasn't just her undulating pelvis that set my blood on fire. She also possessed a vast, intoxicating stillness, great depths in which I swam without drowning thanks to her siren's body. Her spirituality was religious but enhanced by fetishism. When she put her rosary away, she would wait for the right moment, particularly at night, to get out her amulet. I had to accept her need for prayer and her hours of adoration. She devoted a great deal of time to that. Consequently, my time was spent on her beliefs, overt and secret. We ended up becoming inseparable. My heart against hers created the desire for it to last and grow, and for our destinies to be united. Yet before we could marry, Sabrina asked me to see the fetish priest. He had a "bad feeling" about our union and said I had to "cleanse myself of all demons." I used to frequent cemeteries before I met her. During that period of my life, I robbed graves. I stole luxury caskets and left the bodies there. I was never ashamed of it. I had to survive and my adoptive father hadn't been in touch for a long time. So, with a few accomplices, I stole coffin after coffin, flower wreaths and all. The caretakers knew us and, for a fistful of money, would help us rob the newly buried. We were called the Robbers of

Rest and if there was one thing we lacked, it was sleep. We would dig up the graves late at night, then sell the caskets to slimy businessmen. I stopped those activities when my adoptive father started sending me money again. To Sabrina's mind, a robber of rest remained one. I had to undergo an exorcism to expel the evil spirit that was merely waiting for the ideal time to make me pay for my countless incursions into sanctuaries. Personally, I didn't believe in that and refused to go along with such stunts. Sabrina threatened to break up with me because of my many blasphemies. I finally gave in so I could do what had become most dear to me in the world: to marry her. I thus agreed to see a "specialist" who, in the middle of the night, far from any living soul, uttered his incantations. Then came the scarifying of my back. The expert fingers, the biting blade. The unctions trickling as the tears of blood dried, all to the sound of interminable prayers.

After the exorcism rites were completed, we married in a church in a populous neighbourhood. I put my ring on her finger and took the one she offered me, happy to conclude my not-so-glorious past. We had six months of incomparable joy. I basked in her breath, drawing in air my own lungs could not provide. I walked in her shadow in the vain hope of blacking out the universe like a solar eclipse and delighting in her inner light in astral darkness.

Sabrina was the first one to show signs of the affliction invented to deter sweethearts. She lost weight, grew weaker each day, and languished before my very eyes. Once certain of the verdict, she faded at lightning speed. It grieved me to see her passing away. She was no more than a wilted branch whose buds would never blossom.

I buried my wife in one my finest stolen caskets. I laid my love to rest with her cross and her amulet since everything that brought me misery lay between those two irreconcilable poles. It was money from grave robbing again that enabled me to come to this country to sort things out with my adoptive father. He died before I could do so. His stingy wife, that *maboko béton*, prevented me from attending his funeral by refusing to pay for my plane ticket from Toronto to Vancouver. Her son Ryan, who lives in Toronto, promises every week to come and visit me.

165

But he never does. He'll get here too late and, a little like the Canadian troops in world conflicts, he'll be ill equipped to face my reproachful gaze.

Now you know my terrible secret. You finally know why dying from the affliction inevitably decimating sweethearts is the least of my worries. I want to be with Sabrina as soon as possible. She managed to convince me through her steadfast faith in Christ and the occult that the dead are never dead. On that and perhaps on that alone, Christians and animists agree.

Farewell, Schweitzer, doctor of the tortured.

Your friend,

WHO

XXXIII

Living First and Foremost

APOLLINAIRE SAT IN the car holding the letter, immersed in thought. He was silently assessing the extent of his weakness. It had taken the letter from WHO for him to realize how much he wanted to live. Life had value despite the contempt of supervisors like Jacques Dorion and the refusal of the system to give him back his vocation. Life was worth living for love, without hatred.

Adèle's words and those of Colette suddenly seemed to make sense. In their anger and raised voices, he could decipher messages of love. He still had the opportunity to stop associating with dangerous people and seeing patients at night. He still had the chance to regain control of his life, take Adèle in his arms and wipe Anne's tears away. WHO, however, had painfully reached the last page of his life. He was awaiting the spectre of death, convinced that he would thus be joining his beloved.

The doctor felt the need to act as quickly as possible. He had to start altering his course that very moment. He glanced at his watch. It was two o'clock in the morning. What could he do to prove to himself that he was going to change? It was the middle of the night and he couldn't keep the engine running indefinitely. He no longer wanted to sleep at Colette's. That seemed impossible now. He didn't have to take refuge at the home of the person who was trying to save his marriage. He would save it himself. He decided to call Captain Koumba and return Philibert's car. He leafed through his wallet and drew out the number. Without giving it another thought, he stepped out of the cab and walked confidently over to a phone booth nearby. After three rings, a sleepy voice answered.

"Hello?"

"Captain?"

The person did not reply. Yet Apollinaire was sure it was the captain's voice he had heard.

"It's Apollinaire."

Another silence.

"I don't want to see you anymore. I don't want anything else to do with you. I won't be going back home. Ever."

He hung up, satisfied. He felt better already. He couldn't continue seeing people at night. He increasingly feared the consequences of associating with Koumba and treating people illegally. He no longer wanted to be outside his life; he wanted to be in it. His decision was irrevocable. He was finished with distributing condoms to prostitutes and fighting more and more violently with his wife.

The light of day was awaiting him somewhere, the sun resplendent on the pristine snow. He had to learn how to listen to his inner voice again. The one that told him he was fortunate to have a wife who loves him and a daughter who falls asleep in his arms. Anne's smile stirred his heart. Or should he call her Nyngone? He no longer saw any objection. The main thing was to strive for harmony. Could he forget he was a physician? He didn't know. But he would do all he could to be happy.

He drove slowly over to Philibert's apartment. All he could think about was returning the keys. Everything was going to be different. He had to seize the opportunity to live while there was still time. Once at this friend's, he turned off the engine and he felt his chest tighten as he locked the car door. After all, he had spent a great deal of time in this vehicle. He walked through the parking lot, looking back from time to time. At this ungodly hour, he had to be vigilant. Instinctively, he checked to see if anyone was following him. No one.

XXXIV

Philibert's Trouble Sleeping

APOLLINAIRE PRESSED THE buzzer and a voice, hushed but alert, asked who it was.

"It's me. Did I wake you up?"

"Schweitzer! You're joking! Where have you been? Come in."

The question intrigued the doctor. Why had Philibert been looking for him? He hoped nothing serious had happened at home. He entered the building, and his friend poked his head out of his apartment door. Apollinaire saw his pate, with yellowish reflections from the dirty hall light, and then the sparkle in his eyes —the fifty-year-old showed no signs of fatigue. As usual, Philibert addressed him in the national language of their homeland. They shortened their greetings, and his friend motioned him to the couch still bearing the plastic cover.

"Have a seat."

Philibert was wearing a *pagne* like in Africa. Tied in a knot around his waist, the brown bland-patterned fabric hung down to his skinny calves.

Something to wet your whistle?"

Apollinaire replied that he wasn't thirsty.

"We have to raise a glass of the palm wine from back home. The next time you come, it'll be gone."

"Okay."

"Flora!"

His wife did not answer.

"Flora!"

"Mmm."

"Bring us some of that good wine from back home. Schweitzer's here."

He turned to his friend and lowered his voice. "These young women sleep like babies."

Apollinaire made no comment. He wanted to know why his friend had been looking for him.

"I called your apartment. Colette told me that you were at her place. I know things have been heated between you and Adèle. I'm not worried about that."

Apollinaire waited impatiently for him to go on.

"When I called Colette's, there was no answer. I knew I shouldn't call your place again because your wife would've panicked."

"What's going on?"

Flora entered the room wearing a *pagne* that covered her from her chest to her ankles. Her hair had been hastily wrapped in a scarf. Philibert turned to his wife with a grin.

"This is just like my wife. See how she spoils us? This is nice, Honeybun."

Apollinaire couldn't help but give a slight mocking smile. His friend liked mushy terms of affection. The young woman went back to bed without a word. Philibert went back to what he was saying.

"Nicéphore assaulted his wife."

Apollinaire jumped, caught completely off guard.

"I wanted to tell you since you know her fairly well."

"Was she badly hurt?"

"No, but she does have a broken arm."

"How do you know Nicéphore did it?"

"I just know, that's all. It happened last night and everyone's been talking about it. Three of our countrymen called me. They had details as if they'd been there."

"Where are Marcella's boys?"

"At the women's shelter, with her."

The doctor shook his head, looking guilty.

"Don't be so down, Schweitzer. Nicéphore's a wife beater. The guy's violent. What do you want? You can't be everywhere at the same time."

"I should've helped her before things got out of hand. He must've caught her when she was leaving the apartment with the children."

"He got home just as she was getting into the cab. He saw them, and hit her right there on the street, in front of the kids."

"I was right. Fear only begets fear."

"What? What are you talking about?"

"He's afraid of me. I managed to talk to him in front of Captain Koumba. He was petrified, and now he's gone and beaten up his wife."

"You're crazy. He could come and slit your throat. He knows where you live. He could turn up at your place with a knife or his head."

"His head?"

"Yeah. The people from his region can kill with a head butt. They're experts. Apparently that's what he did to Marcella. Bam! Right between the eyes. But she managed to protect herself with her hand. It's true," added Philibert, whispering. "Those people are powerful. They eat their paternal grandfather's heart when he dies. That's how they get such hard heads."

"You forget that I'm from the same place as Marcella and Nicéphore," said the doctor, straightening up and looking irritated.

"Yes, but you spent a lot of time in the capital. City folks don't believe in those things. I grew up in a village. I'm telling you, it's all true."

"I don't pay any attention to such nonsense."

"But . . ."

"And Nicéphore? Was he arrested?"

"Yes, but he's out now, waiting to appear before a judge."

The doctor set his glass down and announced in a neutral tone, "I've come to give you back your taxi."

Philibert did not reply. He knelt in front of his sound system and slipped a CD into the player.

"Good thing. That's why I was looking for you. I've decided not to sell the cab. I'm going back to work tomorrow."

"Ah, finally! Some good news. In any event," added the doctor, "I was going to tell you to forget about Captain Koumba. I don't want to deal with him anymore. No more Scrabble games. It's over."

Philibert pressed the "play" button without reacting.

"So you've dropped your plan of becoming a businessman."

"Yeah. I think that if Flora works, we can pay off my debts in the next five years. As long as we're not extravagant."

"Does she want to work?"

"Yes. We talked about it and she said, 'I can see that you're not rich, you know. I'm not blind. Your apartment's a dump.' And I said, 'Yeah, it's a dump. But it's mine.'"

"I guess she was disappointed. She must have asked if she could go back to her parents."

"No, not at all. She told me she couldn't go back. She wouldn't be welcome. What could they do with a divorced daughter? Men would avoid her."

173

"Do you love her?"

Philibert stared into space, embarrassed.

"Africans today. All you ever talk about is love."

Apollinaire regretted asking the question. He knew his friend would never admit that he was in love with Flora. Of course it made no sense. But for Philibert, admitting he was in love was emasculating; it was like admitting he was weak. He was from a generation that didn't talk about love out loud.

Philibert changed the music to a CD by Francis Bebey and sat back down.

"I couldn't sleep tonight because I found out someone died."

"Who?"

"Francis Bebey."

"Really?"

Bebey's voice reached the two friends from the great beyond.

XXXV

African Laughter

APOLLINAIRE AND PHILIBERT sat listening to the song *Agatha*, heads bowed in a sort of wordless communion. They were soaking up Bebey's lyrics, a tragicomic story typical of the artist, about a baby who didn't have the same skin colour as his family. The song recounted the woes of Agatha's black husband, puzzled by why his son wasn't developing the dark tone of his people.

The doctor lifted his head, his eyes meeting Philibert's amused gaze; they exploded with laughter at the same time. They'd regained the laughter of their boyhoods. Negro laughter. Bebey had that kind of humour—complicit and contagious. In the same frame of mind, they listened to *Si les Gaulois avaient su* and *La Condition masculine*. The music, imbued with good-natured wit, eased their worries and transformed their fears into a glimmer in the tunnel. They felt like hoping before the idea even crossed their minds.

XXXVI

Reconciliation

APOLLINAIRE ARRIVED HOME after sleeping on his friend's couch for barely four hours. He had wanted to be sure to wake up before Adèle left for work.

Colette saw him come in, yet continued feeding the baby in her high chair. She seemed to be in good spirits, but tried to look less cheerful.

"She missed you," said Colette.

Anne broke into a broad smile at the sight of her father. Apollinaire walked over to his little girl and hugged her, pleased to see her looking so happy.

"Adèle's in the bedroom."

Apollinaire turned to go into their room, then back around to face Colette.

"What are you waiting for? Go and see her. If you wreck everything, you're on your own with your problems," she warned, in a tone more friendly than threatening.

The doctor opened the bedroom door and found Adèle combing her hair. The couple froze for a few seconds. Apollinaire took her hand holding the comb and kissed it. The comb fell, but they paid no attention. Adèle's lips were quivering, her eyes filled with tears.

"You have to forgive me. I've been a fool. I've been ruining my life and hurting you. I'm done with seeing people at night."

Adèle ran her fingers through his hair and pressed her lips to his. Standing on her toes, she whispered in his ear, "I hardly slept last night, I was so worried. You'll always be a doctor to me, but don't let this new life destroy us."

"I won't," he murmured. "You've supported me for so long. Now it's my turn to show you how much I love you."

"I know you love me, but I want you to join me."

"How?"

"I've resigned myself to many things. I know I'll never be a nurse again and I liked my profession. Now I work as a chamber maid with the ex-wife of a former Guatemalan minister. That's Canada for you. A race without a referee."

"Doesn't that upset you?"

"Yes, but I came here to be with you. I made a choice. All I'm afraid of is losing you. The important thing is for us to be together. And, besides . . ."

"Besides what?"

"I've been offered a better job at the hotel. I think I can move up in that place. My boss really likes my work."

"Why didn't you tell me?"

"When could I have told you?"

Apollinaire nodded softly. "You're right. But I promise . . ."

"No, don't promise now. Tell me tonight. I have to go to work."

In a tight embrace, they gave each other a long kiss to seal their reconciliation. As Adèle went to leave, Apollinaire held her by the shoulder.

"I'm not proud of what I did back home."

177

"I shouldn't have reacted the way I did. I was shocked when I found out all those things. I should've asked you about the rumours. I'd heard you'd been involved in political business back home. We need to talk about that. But I understand a lot of things now."

"What do you mean?"

"Sometimes you seemed very far away when we were together. Then there were the nightmares. You don't seem to have them anymore, but you were plagued by them for a while."

"Adèle, I didn't have a choice."

"I know. I'm not judging you. They could have killed you. I'm just happy I escaped with you."

Apollinaire took his wife in his arms again. "I'm going to get through this," he said, his eyes on hers.

"I know."

They remained in each other's embrace without a word. Anne's crying brought them out of the room.

"She wants her father," announced Colette.

Colette was gently rocking her against her chest and walking round and round the living room. Apollinaire and Adèle went to her.

"I think you have to go to work," mentioned Colette.

"Yes. I have to run."

"Me, too. I have to leave," said Colette, handing Anne to her father.

He took his daughter in his arms and caught Colette's eye.

"I don't know what to say."

"Don't say anything, Apollinaire. I'm glad you came back."

The women departed, leaving the doctor clasping his daughter. He gave his little girl a bath and walked around the basement with her until she fell asleep in his arms. It wasn't until he put her down in her crib that he stretched out on the couch himself, exhausted. He closed his eyes and fell into a sleep so deep that he didn't hear

Fatima come in. She tried to be as quiet as possible, but before long he awoke. He was glad that she had disturbed him because he, too, had to go to work.

XXXVII

Quick Exit

IT LOOKED LIKE it was going to be a nice day. It wasn't as cold, and the people waiting for the bus seemed to be in good spirits. Apollinaire had picked up a copy of the neighbourhood newspaper, the one to which Kevin Watson contributed. Under other circumstances, he would have read it. At that moment, he felt unable to concentrate. He preferred to watch people amble by, making the most of the first rays of spring. The line for the bus seemed shorter than usual, as the cold was losing its grip. People chose to walk or stroll, even though it was still chilly out. Once on the bus, Apollinaire sat at the back. Almost all the passengers had found a seat. The driver made four stops before the doctor opened his newspaper.

A small woman in her sixties with greying hair stood up to get off the bus. She had difficulty walking although she was not using a cane. She made her way as far as the driver, then collapsed by the steps just after the bus stopped. Passengers gasped in fear and surprise. The driver stood up and tried to revive the woman by patting her cheeks, but she remained motionless. People stopped talking, silenced by the suspense. The steady tick-tock of the bus turn signal could be clearly heard.

"Wake up, Ma'am!"

Apollinaire looked on, taken aback. He thought the lady had simply fainted. The driver pressed his ear to her chest. While he was doing so, a young woman in jeans left her seat and descended the steps to the back doors, which opened automatically. She left to board the bus behind them. Three other people of varying ages also rushed to the back exit, the front being blocked by the driver and the lady.

"Is there a doctor or nurse on the bus?" called out the driver. "I can't hear her heart."

Apollinaire instinctively stood up, everyone looking at him. In truth, he didn't want to be on his feet. He had been denied the right to answer the call. What was he doing? Where did he think he was going? He imagined the look of surprise on Adèle's face. She would have never understood why he'd ask himself such questions. Wasn't it obvious he should help? A woman lying motionless and no one to come to her aid. This wasn't about practising medicine: it was about performing a civic duty. But what was his country's duty? Who could tell him where his duty started, when he didn't know where that of his country ended? As these questions spun through his mind, he didn't know what to do. He took a few robotic steps, without looking at the woman. For the first time in his life, he wondered why he should come to someone's aid. He took a few more steps and no longer saw a body lying on the floor, but a hazy figure. He quickly exited the bus as if fleeing a crime scene and walked off, shoulders hunched. He had to get away and not think about the choice he'd made. Not feel guilty.

"Doctor!"

Who, in such an indifferent city, could have recognized a doctor tiptoeing away? It was Kevin Watson. The old man was following him, breathless. Apollinaire, preoccupied with escaping the location, didn't hear him. Watson finally caught up with him, his coat open, his hands clasped in pleading. This image brought

181

the doctor out of himself. He didn't hear the old man's words, but he saw the look in his eyes, so distressed, so human.

The driver, alone on the bus with the woman still unmoving, was awaiting an ambulance. The doctor climbed the steps and crouched down. He found that the woman's heart was still beating, although faintly. He had to act quickly. He removed his coat and covered her with it. He was afraid that if her body temperature fell, her blood pressure would drop.

"What are you doing?" asked the driver.

"Leave him be. He's a doctor," said Watson without stepping onto the bus. The driver, with a look of disbelief, let him attend to the woman. Apollinaire gently unbuttoned her blouse and placed his hands, one atop the other, over her sternum. He pushed down, but not too forcefully because that could be fatal. He stopped after fifteen pushes, then gave her mouth-to-mouth breaths, feeling beads of sweat on his forehead. He went back to massaging her heart, his hand clammy, then stopped to see if it had started beating. It had not. He performed another series of pushes, followed by breaths. As he was trying to resuscitate her, he felt angry with himself for having wasted precious time. She had to make it. He applied himself to the task and thought of nothing but performing the manoeuvres effectively. Everything should turn out for the best. He could do it. Yes, he was going to do it.

"Her heart's beating normally," he exclaimed.

The driver, who was watching the scene, expelled a deep sigh of relief. At that moment, the ambulance pulled up, brakes squealing. Two attendants, a man and a woman, climbed onto the bus and took the places of Apollinaire and the driver. Kevin Watson waited at the foot of the steps, an anxious look on his face.

"She's breathing normally," said Apollinaire.

The old man shook his hand for a long time, his eyes joyful. The doctor saw the driver explaining the incident to another employee dispatched to the scene. Apollinaire looked at Watson, finally seeing him. Surprised, he asked,

"What are you doing here?"

"I was driving home when I saw the bus stop and passengers rush off. I stopped out of curiosity and got out of my car. That's when I saw you, and I'd been wanting to talk to you. One of the passengers told me what happened, so I ran after you. You know the rest."

The doctor nodded vacantly. "What did you want to talk to me about?"

Watson removed a manila envelope from a pocket inside his thick coat and said, "I received this letter from an influential government official. He's the member of parliament for our riding. He said he's received lots of letters from angry citizens. They're upset because immigrants from liberal professions aren't getting their degrees recognized, when there's a shortage of qualified people."

Apollinaire remained speechless for a few seconds.

"I wonder who was behind all those letters," he said with feigned naïveté.

"Me," replied Watson, smiling. "The MP wants to meet people like you, wronged by our system of . . ."

"Exclusion?"

"Yes, that's the right word. He wants to set up a kind of parliamentary commission. Isn't that wonderful?"

Apollinaire finally smiled. He found the news encouraging, but for a different reason from Watson.

"I really like that idea. It'd give me a chance to meet other people in the same situation."

"You'd be less . . . isolated," continued Watson.

"Yes. This time, you're the one who found the right word."

Apollinaire felt a hand on his shoulder.

"I wanted to thank you for what you did," said the driver. He wasn't more than twenty. His face still had an adolescent quality about it.

"You don't have to thank me. I shouldn't have gotten off the bus. I wasted precious time."

"The main thing is that you helped in time. I'm sure there was at least one other person who knew what to do, but you're the only one who came back."

The other employee, a portly man with a moustache and double chin, was standing beside the driver.

"This is my supervisor," said the young man.

The man shook Apollinaire's hand and stated his name and title. "I'd like to congratulate you, too. The driver told me what happened. I'd like to get your phone number because the City's organizing an awards ceremony for residents who've performed heroic acts. I'd like to submit your name if you don't mind."

"No, I don't mind."

Kevin Watson immediately declared, "I know this man. He's my tenant and I can assure you that he's very brave."

Apollinaire, the driver and the supervisor burst out laughing. Watson moved closer to the transit employees.

"I have to ask you a few questions before you leave. I write for a newspaper and what just happened is a real scoop!"

The men promised to talk to him as soon as the buses were back on schedule.

"Tell me honestly," said Apollinaire. "Why are you doing all this for me?"

Watson turned his head as if he hadn't heard the question.

"Kevin?"

"My father-in-law was a dentist in Poland."

"Really?"

"Yes. He worked his whole life here in Canada as a grocer."

184

Apollinaire smiled complicitly. "So you know what it's like, not to be able to earn your living from your profession."

"Yes. He was bitter about it," he said, saddened.

"Why didn't you tell me that before?"

"I wasn't sure I wanted to help you."

"Why?"

"My wife, rest her soul, told me how hard her father had worked to support his family. And he managed to do it. So why not you?"

"I see."

Apollinaire understood, because he'd thought the same about Chrisosthome.

"What made you change your mind?"

"You're working hard now. And so is your wife. You deserve more than to just make ends meet."

The two men fell silent, feeling somewhat awkward about so much honesty, so much humanity.

THE DOCTOR MANAGED to squeeze onto a full bus. Looking at his watch, he realized that he was almost an hour late for work. He wasn't worried though: he had asked the double-chinned supervisor to call his employer and explain why he would be delayed. He imagined the look on Abdoulaye's face when he told him about his experience.

XXXVIII

An Unexpected Call

THAT EVENING, AFTER Apollinaire had told Adèle about his exceptional day, the telephone rang. He lifted the receiver, his eyes still glittering with excitement.

"Hello?"

"Hello Doctor. How are you?"

He recognized Captain Koumba's voice. His smile immediately transformed into a grimace of distrust.

"I'm fine."

The doctor signalled Adèle to put her ear up to the receiver.

"You've gotten into some bad habits. It's inexcusable to call people so late."

"I wasn't myself. I should have waited until today," admitted Apollinaire.

"Well that doesn't matter now because I'm calling to say goodbye."

"Where are you going?"

"Back home. My flight's tomorrow."

"I see that the wind's turned again. This time in your favour. I'd like to ask you for one more thing," continued the doctor.

"And it'll be the last. Forget me. I think the politicians have better things to do than to try and find out what's become of me."

"All right. I promise you that. It's just that . . ."

"What?"

"My new boss knows you. You saved his life. Joseph N'Gouma, remember?"

The Stolen Choker, murmured the doctor under his wife's astonished gaze.

"Yes. In the flesh. He's come out of exile in Denmark. He's going into politics now that they've promised to introduce a multi-party system. He wants me to set up his personal guard."

"And you believe that?"

"Of course not. I'm no fool. The Stolen Choker wouldn't miss this chance. He'll have me arrested as soon as I set foot in the country."

A strange silence on the line.

"You're not saying anything, Doctor. Do I surprise you?"

"I didn't expect you to face justice voluntarily."

"When you've had such close contact with death for as long as I have, it doesn't frighten you anymore. We should invent something else. But don't bury me too quickly. I think I have a proposition or two that Joseph N'Gouma won't be able to refuse. After all, coming that close to death sharpens your negotiating skills."

"A cynic to the end."

"*Cynic*. Now there's a word I should have played against you in Scrabble. It's worth a lot of points."

A heavy, almost palpable silence.

"Captain, I let you win at Scrabble."

"It's the least you could have done. I let you live."

Apollinaire didn't have time to reply; the captain had hung up. The doctor replaced the receiver, Adèle looking on, stunned. She hugged him with all her might, and he laid his head on her shoulder murmuring, "the Stolen Choker."

Translator's Acknowledgements

I am particularly indebted to Jeffrey Moore and the participants of his QWF workshop for their invaluable comments on the initial chapters of this translation. I am also grateful to *carte blanche* for publishing the first edition of chapter one, "It's Late, Doctor Schweitzer."

A number of colleagues and friends devoted their time and talent to different sections and aspects of this project. They include Susan Lemprière, Diana Halfpenny, Sheryl Curtis, Shelley Tepperman, Margot Priest and Julie Cohen. My thanks to them for their encouragement and expertise.

Thanks also to my revisor, Lee Heppner, for bringing her critical eye and sharp wit to bear on the entire translation, and to my French-language consultant, Pénélope Mallard, for elucidating many of the terms and phrases in the original text.

Special thanks to the author, Didier Leclair, and to the editor and publisher, Ian Shaw, for their kind and steadfast support in seeing this translation through to completion.

Please visit our website at
www.deuxvoilierspublishing.com

CPSIA information can be obtained
at www.ICGtesting.com
Printed in the USA
LVHW011521200819
628308LV00006B/1004/P

9 781928 049524